FOLLOWER

PETER ANDERSON

Bill & Katy,
Hope you enjoy
this! All the
best.
Peter

LIMBERLOST PRESS
2020

15/500

Book design by Meggan Laxalt Mackey, Studio M Publications & Design, Boise, Idaho. Map illustration by Erin Ann Jensen.

LIMBERLOST PRESS

17 Canyon Trail, Boise, Idaho 83716, *editors@limberlostpress.com*. Limberlost Press books may be purchased from *https://www.limberlostpress.com* or from book retailers. For a complete catalog, please visit the publisher's website.

FIRST EDITION
ISBN 978-1-7342192-0-3

Follower is part of the *Expatriate Trio* by Peter Anderson. The group also includes the novels *Viewfinder* and *Builder.*

FOLLOWER

To Jeanne.

All the places we've been together;

all the places we've yet to go.

BERLIN

PRAGUE

VIENNA

BUDAPEST

ZAGREB

SARAJEVO

DUBROVNIK

KOTOR

BARI

TIRANA

OHRID

KALABAKA

ATHENS

Erin Ann Jensen

Who knows what true loneliness is—not the conventional word but the naked terror? To the lonely themselves it wears a mask. The most miserable outcast hugs some memory or some illusion.

— **Joseph Conrad**

PART ONE

MADRID

1 November, Wednesday

Daniel David Durand stands alone in a church. Before him, three dozen candles scatter among the hundred sockets of a black iron votive rack on a marble table. A stalagmitic terrain of wax drips rises from the surface of the table. Irregular clusters of flames, bunched in small constellations where others' hopes inclined, hang still and burnished in the cold, ancient air.

The light of the candles illuminates his face from below, the black vacancies above his cheekbones, the bridge of his nose, the gradual upward fade of his forehead over its mask of slow fire. His steely beard glitters. His eyes are closed, an exhausted medieval face upturned from a well.

Under his soles, stone slabs bear foot-worn script and chiseled faces. Above him, saints and angels observe from many angles. A carved altar off the transept of the church diminishes into darkness beyond the reach of the little dome of candlelight, writhing wrists and snakes, open mouths with gilded wooden tongues. To the left of the altar in a baroque frame thick as a child's waist hangs a quincentenary painting of Isidore, patron of broken-backed farmers, robed in siennas and silky blacks, larger than life-sized, cracked hands and cobalt veins, among his animals and smoked sufferers, all whitened eyes capsized to an unseen ceiling.

In unison, all the candle flames leap and lean to the right as a door opens off the nave. Sibilant leather slippers on flagstones approach and pass. Two sisters in flowing scapulars and cowls glide by behind the man, cross the nave below the altar, pausing at the centerline to turn, bend and lower their faces to their steepled hands, thumbs to chins, fingertips to foreheads. They straighten and then move again, legless in their habits, and pass through the sacristy toward the convent. Another door of black-riveted oak closes behind them, soft thunder in an abyss. The choir of little flames leans briefly the other direction.

Dan takes a candle stub from a pile in a basket. He ignites its wick against the flame of another, watches it flare and settle vertically; a droplet of wax crosses his nail; the little trail of black smoke wriggles into the emptiness above. He presses the candle with the gentlest touch into an empty socket in the black iron frame. For a second, the fire warms his palm. This is unfamiliar territory for him, a strange land. He waits in chiascuro for a minute before in a whisper he says a name, a girls' name. In his long black overcoat, his hands return to the old havens of his pockets.

From some unplaceable distance, the tower of this church or perhaps San Sebastian or San Nicholas, bells begin. Out in the nave, a few early supplicants have already gathered for Mass in the cool gloom. Sunrise sketches in high flecked blues and crimsons of stained glass. Someone coughs, a book drops on the floor in the marbled chasm, pews creak like bone – sounds of eternal waiting. In the stone cavern, a musky scarf of incense from yesterday's processional, from processionals a half millennium past, lingers among the pillars in the crowded dark.

He clanks a one-Euro coin into the slot of a corroded tin box by the basket of candles. He turns and walks the length of the nave, heels clipping uneven flagstones, past the tomb of Miguel Cervantes which two young vacationers, honeymooners, perhaps, out of place and propriety at the onset of Mass, photograph with glowing blue phones, whispering. Dan flinches past. Outside on the cobblestones, it being a holy day, a heavy woman in an embroidered, sweat-salted vest hands short-cropped roses to entering parishioners. A small ribbon winds each stem.

Though offered, he doesn't take a flower. Instead, as he steps to the street, he draws from his pocket another one-Euro coin. He passes the woman with the flowers and slips the coin instead into the grimed hand of a second, much older woman seated beyond on a curbstone, her little form rising to the level of passing knees, her placement an island in the burgeoning flow of people streaming into the church. Gaunt and angry Roma-featured, she clutches a cloth bag emblazoned on its side with cartoon flowers and Eine Welt in cloudy lettering.

Ascending the narrow street, Dan passes a man standing opposite. The man smokes, watches. He wears sunglasses. He has a black mustache and is dressed in charcoal and black. He glances away when Dan looks at him, and Dan notices this. It is as if, stepping from the old church, the man was waiting for him, and as if Dan has seen him before.

CHAPTER 2

MADRID

1 November, Wednesday

Dan crosses the street and climbs eastward along Calle Lope de Vega. It's a street of a few shuttered shops and many unmarked old doorways. Madrid's graffiti, highly-regarded in some neighborhoods, is not well-represented on this stretch. Some of the steel shop-fronts are splashed with crudities, some just quick, careless sketches, initials and personal grievances.

He turns left onto Calle del Leon and then right again on Calle des las Huertas continuing uphill. The morning sun where it crosses the street casts sawtooth shadows among the slate paving stones.

He angles in the general direction of a café a few blocks beyond Plaza Mayor. A chain of bells on the side door, hammered bronze and the size of thimbles, rings as he enters the café. He cuts through the atmosphere of steam and coffee to the end of the marble counter on its black carved base. Several customers wait there, and more line stools along the leaded windows fronting the street, men mostly, a few women, all in tweedy coats and silk scarves, slim, polished shoes. They chat and sip. It's a Wednesday, but a holiday.

The room is handsome and sleek. Two young, dark-haired women handle the line behind the counter. They wear their

4

clothing tight and well. The taller of the two runs the espresso machine. Her nose is long. She laughs a big laugh frequently and slips out little confidentialities, especially to the men as she rattles their cups into saucers, making each stand a little straighter. She meets their gazes, and being Spanish and well-off, their eyes don't waver.

Dan says hello to each of the young women as he moves past the counter.

"Hi Dan," calls the taller woman, who grabs the heavy brass portafilter handle and empties it with a slap into the counter bin in anticipation of his double cortado.

A woman more his age sits on a stool at the cash register. She's smoker-thin; hard hands and neck, green, gripping eyes. She likewise engages each of the customers as she takes their money. She knows most of them. The tip jar overflows pastel Euro bills.

When he steps up to her, Dan says, "Hello Mariana."

"You should have come by yesterday. I saved some leftovers," she says, wiping the counter where the last customer dripped.

"Cacciatore?"

"Last of the eggplant. Still some good ones around if you know where to look."

"My loss. Maybe I can stop by tonight."

She shakes her head, jingling her necklaces. "I have a date. Come by later. I'll bring something back and leave it in the refrigerator."

When he pulls his thin wallet from the inside pocket of his scuffed and pilled overcoat, she waves it off with a sideways glance.

"Anything fun for All Hallows eve?"

Dan shakes his head. "I've just been walking around all night."

"It's been so cold," Mariana says. "You must be freezing in that coat."

Dan says, "I don't feel the cold so much anymore."

"You must be starving, too. Elise," Mariana calls turning to the girl behind the pastry case, "some churros." She turns back to Dan. "The stomach rules the mind," she says.

He slides his plate of churros and chocolate on the marble counter, his coffee, and steps aside to allow other customers room at the register. Then over the clamor, Mariana says, "They're here again," looking over his left shoulder.

"I'm going to talk to them this time," he says, wiping his mouth with a napkin. "I always did enjoy a party."

"Don't," says Mariana, "they may be police."

But he turns and carries his coffee cup to a table where two men in overcoats sit with espresso cups and empty saucers littered with pastry crumbs and crumpled sugar wrappers. One is blank-faced, the other clearly startled when Dan approaches. He pulls back a chair and sits down just as they both stand up.

"I'm told you've been asking about me."

The blank-faced man is first to collect himself. He's taller than the other.

"Are you Daniel Durand?" He reaches a hand to shake. "You're a difficult man to track, Mr. Durand. We've been looking for you." Both men, the taller and the shorter, reseat. The taller man slips off his overcoat and straightens his tie. Dan sips from his coffee cup and then sets it on the table.

"How may I help you?"

The taller man reaches below his thighs and with an intimate scrape across the steel floor draws his chair closer and leans forward resting the pads of his hands loosely on the table, thumbs erect.

"I am Mr. Tranchard. This is Mr. Franco. We've been looking for you because we'd like to offer you a job." After a silence, he continues. "We think you may be the right person, and we think you may be open to the idea of simple and lucrative employment."

Dan glances to the ceiling and back down. "Okay. Why am I the right person, and why do you think I would want employment?"

Franco is bald-shaved, tanned, with two swerving veins running up his forehead. The collar of his black turtleneck is high and tight. He coughs, smirks, looks down at the floor. Tranchard clears his throat. His cold eyes flick to Franco for a moment. Tranchard wears a trimmed beard which he now reaches for with his fingertips. His round black eyeglasses are slightly crooked on his face, as if from impact, which makes him seem to have one eyebrow cocked.

"I hope you don't mind if I continue to speak in French," he says. "I am clearer in French than in Spanish."

"Use Walloon, if you prefer," Dan says in French.

"Ah. You noticed. My accent?"

"Also word choice. *Dejeuner* instead of *petit dejeuner*. That sort of thing. *Bondjoû* instead of *bonjour*."

Tranchard smiles thinly. "Then I will address your second question first. We've come to understand that because of the situation of your status, it has been difficult for you to find and keep employment. That's unfortunate for a man of your caliber, but hardly unexpected given the circumstances which brought you here. True?"

"I'm not doing badly."

"Perhaps. But any of us could benefit from a quick infusion of cash. That's one of the things we have to offer. Please let me tell you about our situation. There is a person who will be traveling across Europe soon. We do not know where. We need to track this person's movements."

"I see. You want someone to do something illegal. I have enough problems," Dan says, pushing his cup away.

"What we would ask you to do would not be illegal, if handled delicately."

Dan shakes his head. "I'm just a guy trying to make it one day at a time."

"You are a guy who once had everything. Now you have nothing. Are you willing to leave it at that?" Tranchard's eyes are suddenly stainless. Franco, not a French-speaker and thus not grasping the dialogue, notices the change in tone, and he looks up from the tabletop.

Tranchard draws a long breath. His eyes half-close behind his lenses, then re-open. He sighs and resets his hands on the table, palms down. The sudden excited barking of a dog that a customer has brought into the café, and laughter from the clientele, don't distract the three men.

Tranchard reaches into an inside coat pocket and brings out a folded envelope. From the envelope he slides a printed photograph of a painting and hands it to Dan.

"As you know, valuable things can be lost. What you see is a photograph of a very valuable thing. It is a painting by René Magritte. One of our greatest Belgians." He pauses, as if to let this sink in. "A small painting, and perhaps not one of his better-known, but as you can imagine very valuable nonetheless. It has been taken. It belongs to my client. I am his attorney." As he appends this last sentence, his eyes rise behind his round glasses with a glance suggestive of practiced legitimacy.

Dan studies the photograph for a minute. It depicts a floating woman, a dog, some trees centered in the view. Then he straightens and looks at Tranchard with a placid face. Tranchard watches him, sighs and scoops up the photo.

"We are not sure who took the painting. But we believe that an associate of my client was involved and assisted the thieves. Indeed, the associate was a trusted favorite. Trust has been betrayed. We think the subject is leaving Madrid to go to the person who has the painting. We think the subject may be headed east. We need to track this person to confirm our suspicions about the thief. The subject will lead us to him."

"So call the police," Dan says in English. Franco has been sitting back in his chair, but at this comment he stiffens and his face closes. Dan takes in this change in posture without moving his eyes. He gazes at Tranchard and smiles slightly. "Or perhaps edifying the police is not a propitious avenue," he says, consciously or otherwise dance-stepping into Tranchard's style.

Trachard is unmoved. "Unfortunately, it is against my client's wishes to bring in the police at this juncture. There are awkward matters having to do with insurance and his ex-wife and his board of directors and certain financial statements that have been made. We are keeping this a private matter. I'm sure you understand how things work."

Dan looks thoughtful. "People often say 'I'm sure you understand' when they're saying something that cannot be understood." He straightens in his chair and draws a long breath. "In any case, the more interesting question to me right now is why you have decided that I am the one for this task."

Tranchard reaches into another coat pocket and draws out a manila folder. From it he takes several sheets of paper stapled together. He studies them in silence.

"You were with the Canadian Security Intelligence Service for fifteen years," he says and looks up at Dan over the tops of his glasses. "You did covert investigations. You gathered information on activities which threatened the peace and well-being of your country. You were a spy, in essence, but a very well-respected one. You were awarded the organization's highest honors. You oversaw many operations. That is until the issues arose."

Dan remains silent, watching him.

Tranchard continues, leafing through the pages. "Royal Military College of Canada, summa cum laude. Rhodes scholar. At Oxford, you read Indo-European languages." He looks up at Dan over his glasses again. "I don't even know what that means," he says. He looks back to the page and continues, "PhD from the Sorbonne. It says here that you were on the Canadian Olympic team in 1992 in Barcelona. But it doesn't say in what sport. What sport did you do, Mr. Durand?"

"Sailing."

"Ah. Sailing. That perhaps fills in some other blanks."

Dan lifts his cup and tilts it to retrieve the final sip. He sets it back on the table. "Where did you get this information."

Tranchard waves a careless hand. "Some, you know, can be found with simple searches." He makes a motion with his index finger as if clicking a mouse.

Dan says, "You need someone followed."

Tranchard folds the dossier and puts it away. "Precisely. We need your special talents, Mr. Durand. Follow someone without being spotted. We need to find out where the painting has gone."

"Surveillance. Not simple," Dan says. "Surveillance is a high-tech enterprise. I'd need a team with specialized training and equipment. That was never really my area. I spent some time in the field at the beginning. But mostly I sat in offices listening to phone conversations, reading emails, looking at websites. I translated for meetings and interviews. Interrogations, sometimes."

Tranchard waves both hands gently, stemming a flow. He says, "You were more than just a translator. In any case, high-end surveillance isn't what's requested. We just need someone to follow the subject, let us know where the person goes, if the person meets anyone. We do not expect you to intervene physically in any way. A low-profile stakeout."

"Given that your client doesn't wish to report anything, tell me more about why you are so interested in this Magritte."

Tranchard's forehead wrinkles for a moment and then flattens again. "A Belgian master, Mr. Durand. A Walloon. I am a lover of artwork and a patriot."

Dan's eyes move from fallen leaves on the steel floor to sconces on the leftward wall. "Others have more skills than I do at this sort of thing," he says. "Of all the people in Madrid, why me? Why don't you just follow the person yourself?"

"Ours is a small, familial group. The person knows us all well. We would be spotted immediately in a crowd."

"Well, there are other investigators in Madrid who are actually in the business of following people. Professionals."

Tranchard's expression sours. "Madrileños," he says in dismissal. "But we serendipitously ran across your dossier, Mr. Durand, and it immediately struck us that you present a superior intersection of qualifications. You are a master of languages, and our subject will likely move among them, especially with eastward travel. And we have come to understand that in the not-distant past you have been involved in some enterprises that, shall we say, would be shy of daylight."

Dan relaxes against the seatback.

11

"You have a reputation as a good, proud man," Tranchard continues. "But it seems you have been willing at times to undertake tasks which fall into grey areas. The matter of the diversion of grocery shipments to homeless shelters, which made such news last summer. We were told you played a significant part in that. And the disappearance of a large group of refugees from Africa who had come into the country illegally. One day they were in a camp preparing for deportation. The next day they vanished. Those tasks involved careful watchfulness – surveillance, of an informal sort, in other words – on your part. You have practiced for the job we are offering. We have spoken to people, Mr. Durand, people who know you well. They admire you. But as admirers sometimes do, they have also divulged things to us that, brought to the attention of the authorities, could cause you grave difficulties, especially given your immigration status and, shall we say, associated problems."

This, too, is met with silence from Dan.

Tranchard leans forward on his seat and with effort softens his features. "I should add, since we are speaking of motivation, that you will be paid well."

Dan watches him for a while and then says, "Describe want you mean."

"We will provide a retainer of five thousand Euros upon your agreement to undertake the assignment, simply to ensure you know we are serious. We will pay your expenses. To accomplish that expeditiously, we will provide a debit card that you can use to withdraw cash, up to four hundred Euros per diem. You can withdraw the whole amount each day, if you wish, and what you don't spend can be extra compensation. Then we will provide an additional stipend of five hundred Euros per day for each day that you provide your services, defined by providing acceptable daily reports about the subject's whereabouts. This second per diem will be paid to you in a lump sum when the job is completed. Finally, we will provide a bonus payment at the conclusion in the amount of five thousand Euros. So, you may anticipate that your compensation will be at least twenty thousand Euros, even if the job takes less than a couple weeks. This should help you get back on your feet, as the British say."

"I don't think it's the British."

"Perhaps the Americans, then. They're always regaining their feet."

Dan sits quietly for a few minutes. The two men let him sit. Franco watches Dan carefully. A skull-and-crossbones tattoo on his wrist emerges from his sleeve. He repeatedly stretches his cuff over it.

"I'll have to think about all of this," Dan says.

Tranchard places his hands together and then lowers them, palms outward, the gesture of a pasha granting a favor. Then he presses his glasses upward with a fingertip. The three of them remain seated in the clamor of the café for a minute. Then Dan moves as if to stand.

Tranchard says in English, "You are married, Mr. Durand?"

Dan stops.

"Where is your wife, Mr. Durand?"

"In Paris, last I heard."

"And your daughters?"

"Your information is outdated. I have only one daughter. Paris also."

Tranchard says nothing further. He nods slightly. The mention of family is left hanging. Then his face reddens.

"Allow me to offer a token. To thank you for the conversation." He reaches into another internal pocket and produces a long, tan billfold. From it he selects a packet of bills pre-counted and held in a steel clip. He holds the packet out to Dan with his fingers over it, shielding it casually from café eyes, and after a pause Dan lifts a hand and takes it. Franco's eyes track the money as it changes possession. Dan slides the packet into his jacket pocket. Then Tranchard and Franco stand.

"Shall we talk again tomorrow morning? Perhaps at ten?"

The two men turn and maneuver among tables and exit through the side door of the café.

Mariana is at Dan's side immediately. "What's up?" she asks. She is tightly knotted.

"I'm not sure."

"Who are they?"

"I don't know. Maybe gangsters. Maybe police. Maybe dishonest journalists. Maybe honest lawyers."

Mariana says, "What do they want?"

Dan considers this question for a minute. "I'm not sure what they want," he says at last. "But I can pay for the coffee now."

He sits at the table for an hour, then leaves and goes to his room in La Latina. There he falls onto his narrow bed and sleeps, unmoving.

CHAPTER 3

MADRID
1 November, Wednesday

Dan awakes midafternoon and showers in the little bathroom adjoining his landlady's. He descends five flights from his rooms under the eaves, crosses to a bodega in the street and buys a packet of razors and the luxury of shaving cream. In his bathroom, he shaves off his three-week beard. He studies himself in the mirror, rubs his eyes.

At a store up the street, he buys a new pair of handmade Spanish shoes. His old pair, evidence of years afoot, he drops into a trash can on the street.

The weather front has blown over and the day has cleared to tepid. He walks to Puerta de Toledo and then through the long traversing streets over the gentle ridge and down to the Neptune Fountain. He angles through the plaza on the north side of the Prado past the statue of Goya fronting the cliff of the Ritz.

He visits San Jeronimo el Real, the second time he's been in a church this day, the second day in two decades. He and Angelique were married in a smaller version of this one in Quebec, a nod to their shared backgrounds and apprehensive parents. But like many moderns raised Catholic, their ancient, clawing religion seemed to them like the prospect of death;

15

always there, inevitable, but what's the point of thinking about it?

Inside San Jeronimo, a few people photograph walls and the baptistery. Across the long fascia of the balcony, he reads again and again the benediction etched in Latin. So long since he's looked at Latin, but it's all still there; it comes to him slowly.

A year after he and Angelique were married, they traversed Mexico, pausing in Mexico City for two weeks. They stayed at the old Hotel Bamer, across from the Alameda, with its giant, faded, fin-de-siècle globe taller than a man in the center of the lobby. At that time, they still made love every day.

In the afternoons, they wandered the Zona Rosa shops and galleries, malachite rooms in Chapultepec Castle, ruins of Aztec sanctuaries amid fruit and vegetable markets, the Pyramid of the Sun at Teotihuacan, since climbing it was then still allowed. A tall and beautiful couple, they turned heads. They attended Carmen in the Palacio de Bellas Artes, Leonard Cohen in Salon Los Angeles. And they meandered through the old earthquake-tilted cathedral on the Zócalo.

That was the last time he had been in a Catholic church prior to this morning.

At the edge of the Estanque Grande in the center of Parque Retiro, he watches a pair of large, graceful model sailboats. Two teenage boys with antennaed remote control devices stand a dozen meters away on the stone embankment. They control the boats. Though against park rules, they've surreptitiously lowered the boats into the water over the iron railing. The sailboats race each other slowly in a ghost of breeze descending the lake from the north.

Dan approaches slowly and stands near them, leaning on the balustrade. "You're good sailors," he tells them. The boys reverse the boats and they pull parallel against the breeze along the wall. A pair of ducks paddles away. "Tack," Dan says, "tack now," and the boy whose boat is trailing the other tacks. Immediately his boat blankets the leader and pulls ahead a few feet.

"That's how it's done," Dan says.

That evening, he stands at the upper eastern edge of the great plaza of Sol and simply watches, hands in pockets, for ten, fifteen, thirty minutes. The night sky is florid with city light. He's not been captivated like this for years.

He moves downslope to the base of bronze Charles III and his heavy horse, suspended in the vast space between the bell tower of the Old Post Office and the giant neon Tio Pepe sign in the sky.

Sol, one of Europe's great public squares, living seat of riots, demonstrations, murders, news and gossip, surging protests, New Year's celebrations, victory parades and countless lovers' rendezvous; heaving, seething, breathing Sol. Dan's face radiates.

The Europe of financial managers and project managers, attorneys and accountants, manufacturing and power generation, stocks and commodities, industrial farms and trucking, rail and shipping, endless kilometers of suburbs and exurbs, of seven hundred and forty million human souls – that's out there, the complete cyclorama. But this moment in Sol is the Europe that one loves, and then, in familiarity and the thickets of everyday travail, forgets how to love.

And as if to underscore its bloodlines, on this evening a commotion begins around a crowd near the bowl-like lower fountain of the plaza. A small group carrying *Falange Espanola* banners and Spanish flags yell anti-immigrant slogans. They boil hatred for refugees. A few of them shove Nazi salutes to the surrounding crowd. Some wear helmets. Police surge, some on foot, others on horses.

The larger encircling crowd, some of whom have clearly come to voice countering positions, armed with banners of their own marked with peace signs, crying tolerance, some of whom have just gathered ad hoc, roars back overwhelmingly, swamping the knot of fascists. Forests of swaying fists rise. The surrounded group of fascists compresses in defiance. A few of them light road flares and hold these aloft, symbolic torches. The brilliance of the flares blinds and enrages the eye and momentarily darkens everything around, as symbols can do. The fountain's overflowing bowl hangs a silky curtain of water in the firelight.

From Dan's viewpoint near the entrance to El Corte Inglese, the flares appear a cluster of candles. Since his dawn visit to the Convent of the Barefoot Trinitarians, a deviation has been presented to this man, and his expression belies this re-direction. The scene around the fountain unfolds, the wrong and the right, and the right winning, the inescapable pressure of passion. He murmurs along with the anti-fascist chants. His fists shake in the pockets of his coat, and his eyes are wet.

CHAPTER 4

MADRID
2 November, Thursday

"I thought about this overnight. I don't like it at all," says Mariana.

Dan shrugs agreement. They sit together at a table in the café Thursday morning.

"I don't trust these men," Mariana continues. "Too many questions. Why did they just appear out of nowhere and know all about you?"

Mariana's counsel has always been haven. Dan listens, but taps his fingers on the table. They speak Italian, Mariana's native language, to isolate their conversation.

"It sounds dangerous, Dan. You've worked both sides of the street before, but not like this. You need to make a living, not end up deported. Or in jail."

"I don't trust it either," he says, "but for me it's a door out of nowhere."

They sit together an additional minute. Dan reaches over and places his hand on hers.

"I realize the money is tempting," Mariana says. "But there are other ways to get money. Safer ways."

"How was your date last night?" Dan asks, steering aside.

Mariana looks momentarily confused, distracted. Then she waves a hand dismissively. "Fine. Nice. She's too young for me.

She kept quoting song lyrics I've never heard of. Can you still do it?"

"Do what?"

"Spy on people."

He hesitates. "Not really spying," he says. "If I understand what they want, it's just keeping tabs on where a person goes. Tailing without intervening. I can do that. The crux of the matter will be whether the money actually shows up."

"What if they don't pay you?"

"I run."

"What if the person spots you and comes after you?"

"I run."

"Great," says Mariana. She sighs. "One of the problems is that you may not be coming back here."

"Why wouldn't I come back here?"

"Because if something goes wrong, this is the place they'll look for you."

"Nothing will go wrong."

"If something goes wrong."

"Whatever happens, I'll be back," he says. "I'm not thrilled with it, Mariana. But what other prospects do I have? What's going to come my way? Money isn't life, but it's very helpful in some of the smaller angles of life."

He pauses, but only for a moment.

"I'm thinking of my daughter. The time has come for me to do something. I need to step forward and bring her back to me. I've been drifting far too long."

He speaks this last series of sentences rapidly.

"I still don't like it," Mariana says.

Dan sips coffee and reads. Mid-morning the café door opens and Tranchard and Franco enter. They order and come to his table carrying their cups. Dan nods, and they sit.

"Good morning," Tranchard says.

"Who is the subject?" Dan asks. "And what does he look like?"

Tranchard wears a different knit tie today, this one blue. The tie has a gold dot of a pin just above the cross of his lapels. He adjusts the tie. Franco wipes his nose briefly with his napkin.

"Her. Her name is Agata Svendson."

"What do you know about her?"

"We have an address in Madrid, although she is not Spanish. She is an American."

"Still in Madrid?"

"We believe so." The wind has increased, and when the café door opens, leaves skitter across the floor. Tranchard reaches into his jacket and takes out his phone. He pokes it a few times, rotates the phone to face Dan and lays it on the table face up.

The phone displays a photo of two people, a man and a woman. They sit at an outdoor table on cobblestone pavement under trees. It could be any café on any sidewalk anywhere in Europe. People in the photo wear short sleeves and skirts. Iced drinks glisten on the tables. Most of the people wear sunglasses, including the man and woman in the foreground. In the photo, the man leans back, the woman leans vaguely forward, but not warmly, more as if the chair is uncomfortable. Her face is in proximate profile to the camera. Evidently, the photographer zoomed from a distance. The photo blurs and tilts.

"That's the woman?"

Tranchard nods again.

"Who's the man?"

"We don't know. He may be one of her associates."

The woman is blonde. There is little detail to be gleaned from the photo, save her good, square jawline and cheekbones, her short hair.

"How long ago was this taken?"

"Last June, I believe. Although she has worked for my client, it's the only photo we have of her."

Dan says, "You mentioned that you think she's headed east. What do you mean by east? You see, I have a little problem with immigration. I'm unable to leave the EU."

Tranchard nods. "We are aware of this." He slips a hand into a pocket and brings out an envelope and opens it. He hands Dan a red Spanish passport. Dan opens it. The passport is recent, though not unused. The visa pages show a small number of stamps: Egypt, Morocco, Venezuela. The birthdate, though not accurate, is credible. The photo is of Dan, thin-bearded. The name on the passport is Alvaro Rodriguez.

"We had this made for you. It's not perfect, but it will allow you to travel."

"Where did you get the photo of me?"

"It's just a snapshot that has been improved. It was taken in this café last week. We apologize for the intrusion."

Dan studies the photo. "If the number is fake," he says, "the passport won't work. I'll be arrested."

"The number is not fake," Tranchard says. "The name and number duplicate a legitimate passport. It will not be flagged, at least not during the period you may be using it. The people who made this for us are very good. You understand how these things work."

"You keep saying I should understand how things work," Dan says.

From the same envelope, Tranchard draws a bank card. He hands it to Dan. It is a debit card from a prominent Spanish bank. The name on the card is Alvaro Rodriquez.

"This card will provide access to the account from which you will be able to withdraw the funds as they are made available to you. The PIN for the debit card is the last four digits of the ID number on the passport."

Dan slips the card into the passport and both into a coat pocket.

"I would like the photo, but I don't have a way to receive it," he says. At this, Tranchard gestures slightly to Franco, who digs in a pocket and sets a phone on the table. Dan lifts the phone and clicks it on. Watching him, Tranchard says, "The code is your birthdate. The birthdate on the passport."

The phone starts up. It is simple and empty. Dan looks around on it, opens the contacts list. There are two contacts. One has a name, Agata Svendson, and street address in Madrid but no phone number. The other has a phone number but the name field says Text.

Tranchard says, "In the phone, we have given you the address that we have for the woman in the photo. The other number is how you will keep us informed. You can send text messages to the number, photos if you wish. You cannot call the number. Or I should say, if you do call, no one will answer, and the call will not be connected. You may receive messages from us. But you may not. The phone is a prepaid device with a new number. It's called a burner phone, meant for only one purpose. It is very restricted. For reasons of security, I'm sure you understand, we have programmed the phone so that it can only communicate with the single phone number in the contacts list. You cannot call others with it, nor can they call you."

Dan opens the camera on the phone. There is one photo stored, the photo of the woman and the man in the café.

Dan raises the phone and before they can react he snaps a photo of Tranchard and Franco. In the resulting snapshot, they are startled animals, Tranchard a hound and Franco a cow.

"In case your faces become of interest," Dan says. He slips the phone into his internal coat pocket.

Tranchard collects himself. "Then I take it you accept our proposal."

"As long as the money shows up."

"The first report will be due tonight by 2100."

"It's too late for today. She will have left her home. With nothing more to go on I will not find her in this city."

"Tonight by 2100. Keep the reports as short as possible."

Tranchard stands. He reaches his hand to Dan. They shake. Franco stands also, arms at sides. Tranchard draws another envelope from an internal coat pocket and hands it to Dan. Dan opens the envelope and glances into it: a finger-thick pad of bills. He does not count it but can see they are hundred-Euro notes. Tranchard and Franco turn to leave.

Then Tranchard stops, turns back toward Dan as Franco steps through the side door of the café. He says in a strong Walloon accent very quietly so only Dan can hear, "Follow that woman. Follow that painting. It is very important to us. Be very careful. Trust no one. Things may not be as they appear with these people."

He turns again and leaves the café.

CHAPTER 5

MADRID
2 November, Thursday

Dan's apartment is a bedroom on the top floor of an ancient building on Calle Mediodía Grande. From the street, the building stands narrow and pale yellow. Iron railings on the balconies, especially on the upper floors, need scraping and straightening. Long window shutters split and cracked in the sun many summers ago hang grey and slope-shouldered in their casings. At this time of year and of the afternoon, the sun slants in low through the shutter slats and light slices the dusty air. Pigeons on the outside sill mumble and scratch. From downstairs rise archival food smells and showtunes on the radio, an absence of footsteps, an antique quiet.

The room's ceiling is a frame of dark timbers bearing the adze marks of leather-clad forest workers four centuries past. The undulating script of the wood collects dust and tiny spiders. It's a former servants' quarter. Stairs leading to his room ascend steeply from the kitchen of his landlady on the floor below.

A back door to the kitchen, a delivery portal, opens onto the rear of the building's central hallway, and this is Dan's entry, the kitchen a foyer of sorts where there is always a pot of oxtail soup warm on the stove and bread and fruit piled like still life on the marble counter. His elderly landlady – most of the tenants of the building are very old – is a widow whose young husband was a victim of the White Terror in 1942. She never remarried. Board is not included with Dan's rent, but then he hasn't paid rent recently, either.

This, in fact, is a matter which he now rectifies. He wakes from a nap, bathes quickly at his room's sink and then goes through his small collection of belongings. He eyes each thing, assessing usefulness for the task ahead, sorting into two piles, one to carry with him and the other to stay. Neither pile is large, but the pile to be taken is smaller.

Most of his valuable possessions – a Swiss watch, a German camera – have long since been pawned. He's left with only three tools: an old pair of Austrian binoculars, a pair of nail clippers, and an aluminum pocket flashlight with a dead battery.

He goes downstairs. First, he counts out a small stack of hundreds and tucks the bills neatly under a pear on the counter. He finds a sticky-note pad by the telephone, writes, "What I owe plus a token for your patience. Thank you," and sticks the note on the money.

He descends to the street and to a phone store. He glances over the modern models but asks for a temporary pre-paid phone. They ask to see ID, and Dan shows them the fake passport. They make a copy of it.

He sits in a café and orders a café cortado. On his new personal phone, he calls Mariana's café. Mariana answers. He gives her his new number for the pre-paid phone he's just purchased.

"Good to be able to reach you now," she says. "Welcome back from the shadows, my friend."

He experiments, testing Tranchard's statements about the phone they gave him, the company phone. First, he locates the number of the phone in the ID information and then calls it from his new personal phone. The call produces a recorded message in rattling Spanish to the effect that the number is not in service. Then, using his personal phone, he tries calling the number identified only as Text in the company phone. It rings, but no one answers and there is no message, just an eventual click and then nothing.

He sits forward and clinks down his cup. On his personal phone, he dials Angelique's number in Paris. The ringer buzzes seven or eight times. Then a recorded voice comes on and says slow and shadowy, "Please leave a message." It's her voice, her aloof dismissal voice.

"Hi. Just wanted to say hello and see how you've been doing. I'm still in Madrid. I'm fine. Haven't heard anything in a while, so just wanted to check in. Is your back doing okay? Did Gennie get the classes she was hoping for? Call me if you want. OK, that's all. Bye. I'd like to talk to you sometime. Hope you're doing well. OK, bye."

At a men's store, he buys two pairs of Egyptian cotton underwear, a patterned shirt, a dark scarf. In the window of an adjacent store he sees black-bound notebooks with elastic bands in varying sizes. He buys two small ones and a couple of roller-ball pens. All of this he takes back to his room.

He packs the notebooks, pens and binoculars into a weathered leather shoulder bag, along with a partially-read copy of Italo Svevo's *Zeno's Conscience* in German which someone left in Mariana's café.

He slings on his jacket and his shoulder bag and closes the door behind him softly.

He maneuvers through the streets to the address given him in the phone. It's on Calle Felipe V up from Plaza de Oriente and around the corner from Teatro Real. The entrance door is beveled glass, giving into a small foyer. He steps up to the door. His view into the foyer is fractured and planar. The floor in the foyer is polished black marble. A small panel of brass mailboxes hangs on the right wall and steps depart upward under a grand doorway with carved moldings stage-like on the left.

He walks up and down the street, then circles the whole block. The building is five stories. According to the address, her flat is on the third floor. It may be the apartment facing the street. Thin curtains are drawn. A lampshade glows beyond.

After the clear morning, some gentle weather has crawled back, spreading a tired sky over the old city. A café fronts the street nearby, with some sidewalk tables, and another café just beyond. In the other direction, sunken Plaza de Oriente lays out mazes of sculpted shrubs and disciplined trees, graveled walkways, two fountains, a semi-circle of benches facing the plaza before the theater.

He sits on one of the benches. From here he can view the front door of the apartment. A trash collector in a small electric cart comes along and empties the cans near the steps. A couple drifts by, pausing to photograph each other and the two of them together before a statue in the park, and then head for the cathedral. People enter a side door of the theater, probably employees returning from afternoon break. A woman pushing a stroller calls repeatedly to a small boy who runs ahead. As she passes she glances momentarily at Dan, the scan of a mother animal.

Four African men come through the park slowly. They sit together on the next bench in the row. Afterward another African man arrives. He speaks to the four, but there isn't room on their bench. He approaches Dan and asks the time, baring the back of his wrist to show he has no watch. Dan, likewise, has no watch, but he checks the time on his phone. Then he asks for a cigarette, which Dan doesn't have. The man nods and asks if he can share the bench, sits at the opposite end. He looks at the other men as if they are a club of which he would like to be a member.

The man speaks French but with a Malian accent heavy with the Sudanian Savannah. He tells Dan a little about himself, his family, his prospects. He shares these comments unbidden. Dan asks if he is comfortable in Spain.

"It is not my home," he says. "I left my home and now I have none. A home is not just a place where you have work and family. A home is a place where others want you to be. There is nowhere on earth that I am wanted now, including in Mali."

Since he smokes, there is a possibility that he's afoul of Boko Haram, or maybe he's one of the teeming millions who poured down from the forests to Bamako and hovered there, waiting in their knock-off Nikes and Bundesliga jerseys, queuing to bathe at wall faucets in alleys, looking for any way out of Africa, open to all suggestions.

His name is Edward. They talk at intervals. Dan and Edward are both fearfully skinny men, but Edward is skinnier. At the tips of jointed pencil fingers, his nails arc ridged and mauve from malnutrition. Dan pulls a bag of almonds from his satchel and offers them to Edward.

Dan watches the apartment building across the plaza and up the block. The presence of the other men on the benches with him is in a sense cover. Among them he becomes like them: overlookable.

The prolonged Spanish period between dark and dinner unfurls. Those working still sit in their offices; those not working wait for them in cafés sipping coffee, erasing the slow minutes. The world is chatter, the clinking of glass and china, the swirl of scooters. Building facades melt into purple velvet splashed with

29

abstract golden ovals from streetlamps. The theater suddenly lights like a palace.

Dan asks Edward where he has looked for work. He encourages Edward. He offers to make inquiries to see if he can help, knows that any work will do, sometimes. Dan has scraped a minor living from publishers, ad agencies, web designers, friends of friends, mostly language translation for under-the-table cash payments. He has also taken day-labor jobs when they would come his way, references and tips from people he knows, carrying things in and out of buildings, sweeping. He has not registered with employment agencies because they would ask for identification.

He reaches into his pocket, draws out some bills and gives Edward forty Euros. Edward is damp-eyed. "I will buy a meal for all of us," he says. The other men each shake Dan's hand in solemn silence. He wishes them good luck. The African men leave. They drift without objective, in some form of terrestrial limbo somewhere between a kitchen and dinner in Europe and a slave camp in Libya.

Then Dan stands and moves to the apartment building again. Just as he is abreast of the door, a woman appears in the foyer. She is grey-haired, dressed for the evening. She digs for something in her purse. Dan steps up to the glass door and opens his satchel, pats pockets as if searching for his key card. Before he can locate it, she comes through the door. Dan looks up and smiles gratefully and enters as she exits.

The mailboxes have paper name cards on little brass faceplates. There is no Agata, but there is an A. Svendson on the third floor. The building is quiet. The grey-haired woman has disappeared down the street. Dan climbs marble stairs to the third floor. He sees no security cameras. Her apartment is at the end of the hall. He listens at the door. There is no sound.

He descends. Just as he reaches for the handle to open the door to leave the foyer, another woman appears outside coming from the left. She steps onto the threshold and digs in her black leather purse decorated with steel rivets for her key.

Dan pulls the door open and steps back for her. She looks up, then steps over the threshold and enters. She turns and nods to him. He nods back and smiles. She is red-haired, a shadowy vivid tone of hair. It is cut short and trimmed over her ears and finessed down her neck. She wears a brown coat over a white wool jacket and tight jeans and boots with heavy buckles. Her face is square and deliberate, with boxlike cheekbones, blueish eyes lightly made up. She looks as if someone just told her something pleasant, vaguely amusing. Dan takes all of this in with a quick pair of glances, one after the other, as she passes him and moves down the hallway toward an elevator.

On the street, he takes out the company phone and brings up the photo the two men had given him. The woman he's just encountered is unmistakably the same one seated at the café table in the photo: the square face, the horizontal but soft mouth. The woman in the photo has blonde hair and it's longer. But they said the photo was from some months ago. It is difficult to hold a glimpsed face in short-term memory. After he looks at the photo for a quarter-minute, he re-pockets the phone.

He crosses the street to the nearer café, takes a table. He converses with the waiter for a minute. In the building across the street, lights come on in the third-floor apartment, first in the rooms to the south and then the north. A curtain is drawn open, then re-closed.

Dan waits, reads a magazine, reads a newspaper.

On a few occasions, years ago, Dan was assigned to assist field operatives on stakeouts because it was thought language translation may be needed.

31

The first time, CSIS was tracking the movements of some Russians in Toronto. Another time, they were watching some Brazilians in Vancouver. He sat in cars, in vans, for scores of hours amid stinking and greasy food in take-out containers, cups of thin coffee, chewing and slurping interpolating spells of inane, listless conversation meant for nothing other than burning hours. "How can they do that day in and day out?" Dan asked Angelique rhetorically. "I'll be so happy to be back in my little office, burrowed in."

All this comes back to him as he sits, leafing through articles as hours pass, though the coffee is better, music plays, and no one talks to him.

Customers depart the café. The last waiter is putting up the chairs and wiping tables. Dan leaves and walks up the street to the other café, but they are closing also. He sits on the concrete rim of a planter outside. He watches, but there is no movement in the apartment other than the glow of a television somewhere in the room which comes on, burnishing the curtains blue for an hour, and then goes off. Another hour passes, and Dan does nothing more than stand occasionally because the planter is stony cold. Not long afterward, the lights in the apartment go out. He waits a while longer but there is no sign of further activity.

Dan takes out the company phone and types: "Agata Svendson identified at residence." He sends the text, then stands for a few minutes holding the phone as if considering sending something more forthcoming. Eventually he repockets the phone and walks home.

CHAPTER 6

MADRID
3 November, Friday

The next morning, Dan experiments with withdrawing money from the account. He slides the debit card into a bank machine, enters the number, and pauses to consider how much to request. His expenses promise to be small. But he enters the maximum that Tranchard had indicated would be made available. The machine presents four hundred Euros.

He watches the apartments from his bench in the park. He reads the Svevo, which he's read in the past but long enough ago that the book is as if new and is different than last perceived. At one point, Dan takes out one of his little notebooks and copies a line: *You see things less clearly when you open your eyes too wide.*

The woman presumably named Agata Svendson steps from the front door of the building an hour later. Dan sits in the café up the street from her apartment sipping coffee and crunching churros when she emerges wearing tights, a running jacket, a cap, running shoes. She walks springily down to the park benches in Plaza de Oriente. She limbers for a run, stretching her legs against the benches and the low stone wall. Then she bounds into a quick jog through the manicured gardens and toward the palace and the park beyond.

He cannot follow on foot or by car. He paces up and down Plaza España several times, circles the theater. The issue at hand is whether to report that he lost track of her. He cannot be expected to follow a runner. She was carrying nothing, not even a phone, as far as could be seen. She might have something small, communiqués or other missals, memory media, tucked into discreet pockets. These could be delivered to colleagues at pre-arranged meeting places. None of this could be known by a casual observer, and that is all he was hired to be. He returns to the café and takes a table by the window.

She returns a half hour later, sleek and hot, hands on hips, kicking her legs out to stretch them, bouncing on her toes. It seems evident that she has been running, not lingering anywhere along the way, at least not for long. She still carries nothing. She goes inside and comes out about an hour later, showered and dressed for the late-fall afternoon. She wears a deep red leather jacket and carries a matching purse. Her scarf, black, appears from across the street to be velvet. She wears heeled boots that rise above the cuffs of her tight jeans.

She walks upward slowly on Arenal through crowds, window-shopping, circles through Sol and eventually enters the Stradivarius store. Rather than following, he decides to wait on the street. She remains inside for an extended period. Fearing he has been left behind, he enters the store. A uniformed guard at the door looks him over. He spots Agata on the women's outerwear floor. She is trying on coats before mirrors, and is currently wearing a slim light-yellow belted raincoat, swiveling left and right. He retreats to the men's floor, looks through some shirts, then exits and resumes his wait on the street. She remains in the store for three-quarters of an hour and emerges carrying a pair of gold-printed shopping bags.

She dines alone in a restaurant off Plaza Opera. Dan sits on a bench across the plaza from the restaurant. It is cold, and the crowds have thinned early. He draws the binoculars from the bag and focuses them on her. She sits alone at a table on the terrace under glowing heat lamps which cast her reddish and polished. A waiter opens a bottle of wine and pours it for her. She downs a glass and pours herself another. She takes bites of steak, sips, reads a book. Her legs are crossed; her dangling foot in the black, high-heeled boot bobs occasionally. She tucks a lock of red hair behind her ear. Dan watches the small movements of her hands. Some figures blink through the foreground of his view, and when he realizes that they are a pair of police women he slides the binoculars back into his satchel.

A screen of tall shrubbery surrounds the dining terrace of the restaurant. Dan moves across the plaza and slips toward the alley behind the shrubbery and a thicket of parked scooters. He stops opposite of where she sits in her coat, reading and eating. Just at that moment, she takes her phone from her purse.

From his distance and through the leafy wall, Dan clearly hears her say, "I'm going to Valencia tomorrow morning. I don't know when I'll be back." She speaks in English, moreover with an American accent, at least the snippet that Dan catches. He notices that she has finished the bottle of wine. The waiter clears her table.

Dinner finished, she goes home. Dan watches from his seat on the planter until he sees her in pajamas draw the curtains and turn off some lights. It begins finally, slowly, to rain. Dan moves to his now accustomed table in the café across the street until the last of her lights go out. He doodles in his notebook, withstanding the ennui only because it is temporary. And Tranchard was correct about the motivation of money.

35

Back in his room, he texts: "A.S. going to Valencia AM." A long time passes as he lies on his bed, shoes off, the sound of water running intermittently in the roof gutters. Then they text: "Follow."

MADRID
4 November, Saturday

Before sunrise Dan rises, splashes his face and shoulders, shaves, then goes to a bank machine and withdraws four hundred Euros. As an experiment, he requests a second draw, of just twenty Euros this time, but the machine announces that funds are not available, demonstrating that the four hundred limit is indeed in place, but the simple nightly reports he has been sending apparently satisfy their recipients.

In his room, he packs the underwear and spare shirt into his shoulder bag with the binoculars and notebooks. He zips the passport, debit card and cash into coat pockets. He tucks the phones into opposite end pockets of the bag. Instead of the long, threadbare overcoat he wears his only other jacket — short, dark blue canvas, internal zipping pockets. It's not warm but is comparatively new, a castoff by one of Mariana's customers.

In the café across from Agata's apartment building, he stands behind the pillar and orders a coffee. He asks the barman to break a few bills into smaller change. He reads the morning papers. He orders a pastry. He reads a magazine.

At seven-thirty she exits her building. She's wearing the light-yellow coat and a pale green scarf wrapped and knotted at her neck. Her pants are deep denim, stretchy; the jacket just reaches her thighs. Her shoes are slim sneakers. She tows a rolling bag made of hard silver plastic embossed with wavelike ridges and with chrome wheels. She lifts the bag down the steps and then stands waiting on the stone street. She looks at her phone, scans up and down the street, looks at her phone some more.

Dan calls a taxi company. He hands his coffee cup to the barman, slings on his bag and stands near the door behind the menu board. His taxi arrives before her car, pulling on the cobbles with a squeak of tires. He slides in and tells the driver to start the meter and then wait. Dan sinks low in the back seat since Agata waits directly across the broad avenue from him.

Presently an unmarked car arrives in front of Agata. Dan waits until they have rounded the corner and then tells his driver to follow. He says, "I think she's going to Atocha." "Your wife?" the driver asks, eyeing the mirror. Dan shakes his head. "Ah, your girlfriend."

He comes into the station after Agata and scans for her in the sea of travelers. He walks toward the hallways leading to the front section, the enormous old building like a blimp hangar with its palm forests and koi ponds. She is not on the ascending ramps. Then he crosses back toward the circus of cafés and shops.

He sees her red hair and yellow coat. She's standing at a ticket machine poking at the screen. Purchase made, she aims toward the ramps to the platforms.

Dan steps up to the same machine she was using. He quickly buys a ticket on the 8:30 to Valencia, feeding a fifty into the machine to pay, waiting for the change. He looks after her frequently, but she has vanished into the next hall. With his ticket, he runs to the ramps and ascends to the long hall of platforms.

He reaches the gate and the agent scans his ticket and says, "Hurry."

When he reaches the corner, he sees her boarding a coach toward the front of the train. The doors are closing. A conductor looks up at him irritably. He jumps into the first car. The door shuts behind him with its hydraulic hiss and the train is already moving.

He's at the tail end of the train. He makes his way forward car by car. They move out of the station and slowly through the vast yards, megaliths of concrete apartment blocks fronting rough fencing beyond.

Doors between the cars open and shut as he advances. Dan continues into coach five, moving slowly, scanning over the tops of each row of tall seats for red hair before he passes since he doesn't want to appear in front of her. He reaches coach seven, doesn't see her, coach eight, doesn't see her. Then in coach nine, a first-class coach, he spots her immediately. She is halfway forward in a single seat on the right side of the car.

Dan stops. He retreats to the rear door of the car. His ticket is for a seat far back in the second-class group. But there are two rows of vacant seats in the rear of the first-class car. Conductors seldom check tickets. If they do, he will silently move. He slides into the double seat on the left so that he is four rows behind Agata. If she comes back this direction, to the bathroom or the cafeteria car, he can pull his coat over his face and feign sleep.

Madrid melts into reefs of low dwellings and industrial pueblos threaded by increasingly vacant freeways, and eventually it all changes to small tilled fields, fallow for winter now, churned and disked into shades of burlap between fragments of stone walls and corrugated storage buildings. A folio of foreboding cloud formations splays eastward. Distant ridges wear a blurred lacework of snow. A cross-wind bends smaller trees and tall, tuft-headed marsh grasses encircling algae-stained ponds. He spots a couple of egrets, a heron.

39

He made this journey southeast from Madrid several times in the past, both on fast trains like this one and on slower ones, but time has passed. Now, he views out the train window the grand plateau of central Iberia, the way it unfolds around a traveler like a wake, the desert spreading as if taking flight, and it's not unfamiliar.

The line rises through gently rolling land. The train punches through eyeblink tunnels now at 300 kph, 310 kph, noted on a little screen at the head of the car. Dan's ears close and pop. Desert hurtles by; curving river beds clotted with brush snake past. Scrubby bushes and sedges blur into streaks; likewise, the clumps of gall oak, Aleppo pine, stone pine, seen at a distance.

Far off, blue-baked peaks hover without touching the ground. Grey, dusty jade, alkali silt, ochre, pale butter, coffee – the earth sketched in Med skin tones evokes comparable landscapes, one step above desperate, through which he has passed in Alberta, Wyoming and Paraguay, save for the stray Moorish watchtowers on lonely pinnacles. This landscape bears a face of ancient lament and determination.

Ancient, but also new. Power lines march across hills carrying wires farmer-style under their great arms. Legions of wind generators astride ridges roll past, and a solar reflector installation gleams countless ranks of sky-facing mirrors interlaced with stainless steam arteries. Amid these, abandoned and roofless stone buildings huddle on hand-shoveled hummocks of dirt; narrow scree pathways lead untrodden to thresholds last crossed perhaps five hundred years ago, perhaps fifty, perhaps five.

He closes his eyes. Other train trips, other transitions, unreel quietly, jogged free, perhaps, by the gentle rocking of the coach.

CHAPTER 8

CUENCA
4 November, Saturday

After an hour, the train from Madrid slows. A voice announces its sole stop in Cuenca, midway to Valencia. Dan looks back to the aisle to see Agata standing and pulling on her scarf and her yellow coat. She tugs her silver suitcase off the rack. She moves toward the forward door of the coach as the train glides into the station. Dan leaps up and grabs his shoulder bag. As he steps down from the coach, she has in fact moved some distance down the platform already. Only two other groups of passengers have alighted in Cuenca, old and young couples with heavy suitcases. The conductors have already swung back into the train, which moves away slowly and silently. A row of faces gazes idly out at the people on the platform, not even curiously, blurring into a glassy stream as the last cars pass.

Deep quiet descends except for the sound of rakes being used by some workers on the pitched slope above the tracks opposite and the cries of some stone curlews somewhere over the rise. There's also the clip of Agata's heels as she reaches the escalator into the glass and patina-steel station. Dan follows.

He tells his taxi driver to follow Agata's taxi. The cars meander a few kilometers down into the new town, meaning the early 20th-century town, which spreads across the alluvial fan at

41

the mouths of two deep adjoining canyons, the Jucar and Huécar. The old town, meaning the 8th-century Arab city, hunches on the high spur between the canyons. Some of its buildings famously hang over the precipices bolstered on timbered stilts.

Their two cars, the second a discreet half kilometer behind the first, ascend the wall of the Huécar gorge through the pale smoke of little fires burning fall leaves along the road. Her taxi curves into the cobbled drive of the Parador de Cuenca, a converted 16th-century convent with fortress walls of creamy sandstone. Dan instructs his driver to stop along the short line of parked cars slanting below the footbridge. He can see Agata up the hill and through the cypress trees and clipped shrubbery as she stands from the taxi, talks to the driver for a moment, grins, turns, and with her bag enters the parador.

Dan pays his driver, takes his satchel and moves slowly up the walkway toward the eastern end of the footbridge. The stonework here is the stubbed remains of the Bridge of St. Paul, the five hundred-year-old footpath to the convent from the upper city. He sits on a block of cool chiseled limestone and waits, considering. He lacks an explanation for why Agata left the train here instead of continuing to Valencia. Some change of plans must have emerged after the overheard phone conversation, or she may have been lying to the person she was talking to, or the whole episode may have been a decoy. But for whom, and for what reason? In any case, the stop here could signify a meeting of importance. Watchfulness is advisable.

After a discreet period, Dan ascends the street to the parador. In the lobby empty of guests, a black-suited man with broad tortoise-shell glasses at the reception desk requests to be of assistance. Dan inquires if a room is available. The man asks for how many nights, but Dan is not sure. "One night, maybe longer," he says, and although an eyebrow rises, it is the off season and in any case Cuenca is no stranger to odd, itinerant visitors with limited luggage. Dan asks for, and receives, a room overlooking the bridge. He shows his passport and the desk clerk enters the number in the database.

The room is large. It costs much of his daily expense allowance. It feels like something from a Bond movie, carpet and wood, missing only a distraction wearing pink suede boots and an orange skirt. He sits on the bed, sinks into its featheriness, a bed unlike any he's sat upon in years. He opens the iron clasps of the carved wooden interior shutters, and the inner windows and the outer windows. The outside air shocks, like diving into icewater. He stands face-out into the world for a time. Then he pulls the binoculars from his bag and surveys the scenery: farms along the winding road in the Huécar gorge two hundred meters below, stone houses and barns built into and wrapping around monolithic cliff-fall boulders, a motorist, a bicyclist, some sheep in a pen, a stooped man inspecting the axle of a wheelbarrow. Pedestrians cross the foot-bridge, their footfalls and laughter audible across the silver distance. They pause singly and in groups for photos.

As he traces the slender bridge with his binoculars, he sees the yellow coat and red hair. Agata is crossing the bridge away from the parador heading toward the city. She's already approaching the metal arch at mid-point.

By the time Dan reaches the bridge Agata has vanished up into the ancient town, and by the time he reaches the plaza he is winded from running.

"Excuse me," he says in Spanish to some people standing on the steps of the cathedral, "did you see a woman in a yellow coat pass here?" He repeats in English this time but receives the same vacant response.

She can only have gone uphill or downhill. Or she may have gone into the church. She walked like a sightseer, not someone destination-bound. He turns and ascends the oblique steps into the cathedral, purchases a four-Euro ticket and enters squinting. And as if beckoning him, the first thing he spots in the dim distance near the end of the seven-sided apse is the yellow coat, drifting between columns. Dan glances around, sees the *unum ex septem* insignia near a chapel promising a five-year absolution for a prayer and he inhales deeply the stony old air, tempted.

He lingers near the gift counter fingering saints' postcards and miniature metal Madonnas for the fifteen minutes until she leaves.

In the plaza, she angles to the right and starts up Calle San Pedro past the quadruple-belled towers of San Iglesia. He traces her path up through the town to the ridge above. She dawdles. She takes photos with her phone, and then, standing atop the Muralla de Bezudo takes a shy photo of herself.

She descends through the plaza to the Mangana tower and then circles back. She sits in a café on the upper edge of Plaza Mayor and orders a glass of wine. He takes a table at a café, lower and across the plaza. He is partially screened by an advertisement kiosk and a row of folded umbrellas. Sunlight warms the stone pavement and marble table. The café is sheltered from the breeze. He takes out the binoculars and casually scans the carving of the cathedral, a row of windows. He lowers the glasses to view Agata. She's looking at her phone.

He watches the profile of her face. Her hair curls around her ears and forward to the line of her jaw. She wears small silver earrings. The green-patterned scarf circles her neck and drapes over her shoulder. She's crossed her legs and her floating foot dangles comfortably, the muscles of her calf and thigh visible through the thin tight denim, the cut of a runner.

He has only eaten a roll so far today, and that early in the morning. He orders a hamburger but has only consumed half of it when he sees Agata paying her server. He manages the rest of the burger into his mouth and wraps the fries in a cloth napkin which he stuffs in a pocket. Agata has already crossed the plaza and started downhill. His waiter is not in evidence, so he tucks a twenty-Euro bill under his plate and departs. This amounts to a twelve-Euro tip, but it's the smallest denomination in his wallet.

She returns to the parador. Instead of mounting to his room, he takes a table in the semi-dark in the courtyard under a potted tree and sweeping canvas sunscreens suspended from cables. It is cold and silent but for an occasional scooter rev from far away. A waiter brings him a coffee.

Some young people come into the courtyard and take a table near him for a while, clinking coffee cups. They are replaced by a pair of older couples waiting for later dinner who drink wine and talk in French, catching up. Everyone's breath shows. Dan, chilled in his canvas jacket, reads more Svevo. He copies another line into his notebook: *Complete freedom consists of being able to do what you like, provided you also do something you like less.*

Eventually Agata appears at the bottom of the stairs. She now wears a black coat and black leather gloves and boots. Her coat is thin knit wool. On her head is a maroon beret. She looks around briefly. She exits the hotel and Dan rises to follow.

Agata goes to a restaurant in Calle San Pedro. He checks around the corner of the window. She has taken a table near the back. Only two other tables are occupied. On the walls hang framed paintings of nails and bolts.

He considers the options. Perhaps he should return to Plaza Mayor and wait for her there. Surely she would aim for the parador through the plaza since there is really no alternative route.

One or more of the cafes on the plaza will probably still be open. If not, it offers an expanse of low walls on its lower end where he could lean and wait.

Just then a man walking up the street crosses toward the restaurant where Dan is still standing outside. The man pulls the door and enters. Dan glimpses Agata rising to greet him. She embraces him and they kiss both cheeks. He is silvery, elegant, maybe sixty. He wears small tortoiseshell eyeglasses. He removes a grey flannel overcoat and suede gloves and sits at her table on a chair which the waiter has drawn back for him.

Dan takes out his phone and pretends to be snapping a photo of the menu. He leans to the right past the post and clicks the shutter again. When he looks at it, glassy reflections blank most of the scene. Agata and her companion are a blur within a glow. He steps further right and tries once more, holding the phone toward the window. A waiter notices him and tilts his head with a what-are-you-doing expression. Dan turns and walks away.

He returns to Plaza Mayor and waits in the plaza, taking a seat at the one café which remains open, the same café at the same table he occupied earlier in the afternoon. He drinks deep red wine. He composes a text to his handlers: "A. S. met man at restaurant." He attaches the second photo, which turned out slightly better than the first, and sends it.

He takes out one of the little notebooks and fills a few pages with observations. He tabulates his remaining money. There is no response to his message. After an hour Agata comes through the plaza unaccompanied, holding her coat closed against the chill with one hand, hurrying. She turns into Calle Obispo Valero, descending toward the footbridge.

CUENCA
4 November, Saturday

At the parador, Dan stops by a bookshelf off the lobby. He exchanges the Svevo for a couple of slim Patrick Modiano novels, recent translations in English, discarded by a previous traveler apparently unopened, the sales receipt from a bookstore near Camden Locks in London which Dan recognizes still tucked between the covers. There's also a thumbed James Salter novel about mountain climbing in Chamonix that he's never read and, although it seems unbalanced trading one book for three, he takes it also.

In his warm room, he undresses, wraps in a blanket, sits in the deep leather armchair with its ornate carved armrests and opens one of the Modianos. After a few pages, the book slowly lowers to his knees, but his grey eyes rise to somewhere on the far wall.

He not infrequently lapses into reflection. The trait at once fascinated and frightened Angelique, drew her into sorrow and helplessness. The disintegration of his marriage followed incidents of infidelity on both of their parts, Angelique's seclusion and growing coldness, Dan's bouts with competitive fury, Angelique's impatient superiority, Dan's gloom and finally the death of their older daughter Adrienne.

Adrienne died in the St. Lawrence off the point of Grosse-Isle. Dan was aware of cracks in the bedding of the rudder pins of their sailboat. But the two of them had just finished a sail together around the island in the stout upriver wind. The cracks seemed limited to the gelcoat, and he had seen far worse. The cracks had been there for a while, through a hard season of regattas. A yard hand had even pointed them out when they pulled the boat the previous winter. The transom had swollen, suggesting delamination in the core, the bolts pulling through.

But Dan had spent so much time on racing boats, always on the edge of equipment failure and physical failure, in the slim margin of life between deck and sea. Risk is part of sailing, of everything, and his excitement he found reflected in Adrienne's young eyes. He had told her all was fine, it would hold, even with the wind breaking force 7 that afternoon.

She had looked up into his face, Adrienne with her strong blue-distance gaze, arms and legs like rigging and her hair tied back in a bandanna, wearing a Henri Lloyd offshore foul-weather coat just like her dad's. So proud of her and amazed by her, her anxiety about her first solo sail overwashed by the force of his enthusiasm.

She had pushed off from the dock with that insouciant, jaded air that he always took, astride the cockpit and one foot up on the gunwale, slung the boat out past the breakwater and tacked hard into the wind, alone with only his encouragement. He last saw her face when she looked back at him, one arm on the canted tiller and leaning into the mainsheet, his daughter tall and perfect of line and angle, like him. The sailboat had disappeared around the island and then had cut back into view ten minutes later. Something was wrong, visible over the whitecaps a half-mile away.

He had seen from where he stood in the marina the sailboat veering rudderless toward a tug and barge plowing upriver, the sudden slack in the main as she cut loose the sheet, but too late, his daughter in the boat's cockpit paralyzed, pulling at the iron-hard genoa sheet, he yelling, "Jump,

jump," into the wind, then the hull disappearing in the crushing gap between the tug and thirty-thousand tons of seagoing steel, and then the mast suddenly, also.

After the police boats came slowly back into the harbor four hours later with her body, found under the broken and splintered little sailboat jammed and tangled in the tow cables against the hull of the barge, and they had come to him where he stood in the lee of the marina's shower hut, and after he had given up trying to call Angelique, who so often forgot to charge her phone, neighbors unable to locate her, but instead drove the long miles home into Quebec, walked up the steps into the house and stood there in the foyer.

It all seemed like a moment foretold. As if he'd been preparing for it his entire life. He never stopped preparing for it.

Each moment of his life, seen in hindsight, seems to him a logical and pellucid step from the last, always preventable; all suffering the fault of the sufferer.

In the parador, Dan doesn't sleep. He lies on the bed. He switches on the television, then silences the moving faces. He sifts through a parador magazine, all pouting models and misted happy families. He turns a few more pages of Modiano. Eventually, he opens the cedar shutters. The sun has prepared its coral entry over the escarpment-bound, time-worn city.

CHAPTER 10

CUENCA
5 November, Sunday

The breakfast room of this parador is the former refectory of the convent. It's shortly after seven the next morning. Dan, not having slept nor eaten much the previous day, is ravenous. Buffet tables offer platters of steaming sausages, *patatas Española*, eggs and cheeses. Before he can take a plate, he sees Agata dining by herself halfway up the room. She has taken off her yellow coat, but her suitcase sits by her table.

Dan runs upstairs and grabs his satchel. By the time he returns to the dining room, Agata has left. From the lobby he sees her meeting a taxi on the curving driveway. The driver lifts her suitcase into the trunk. She is putting on her sunglasses.

Dan asks the desk clerk to call a taxi. The morning, like most here, is quiet. Almost ten minutes passes before his car arrives.

He guesses she went to the Ave station. When he arrives, he sees her just entering the building, as if she waited a while on the terrace. She goes straight to the security line. She doesn't stop at a ticket vending machine or office, which suggests that she either purchased her ticket online or purchased it earlier in Madrid in anticipation. She walks to the waiting area at the far end of the building.

Though he's guessed correctly that she's taking a train, he isn't sure where she's going. A train back to Madrid comes through soon after the train eastward to Valencia, and occasional local trains. But he guesses Valencia, and goes into the *taquilla*, where the ticket agent scans his passport as he makes his purchase. Ticket in hand, ten minutes before the train arrives, he stops at a bank machine in the concourse. It dispenses four hundred Euros.

As when leaving Madrid, he maneuvers slowly through toward the front of the train as it accelerates through the hills, eventually reaching the first-class coaches, and there, like a beacon, is her red hair in the farthest forward car. There's no empty seat in coach ten, so he takes a seat in coach nine. He cannot see her from here, but there are no stops until the terminus in Valencia.

The train begins its descent from the Spanish steppe toward the coast. The landscape yellows toward grey and the karst outcroppings tarnish. Agriculture develops. Industry emerges. Descent toward the coast is like traveling forward in time.

They disembark on rain-slick platforms in Valencia. At the vacant taxi queue, Agata talks to another traveler. She shrugs, frustrated. She hurries through to the little bus which shuttles passengers from Sorolla two blocks to Estacion del Norte. There is a taxi strike, Dan learns. He heads for the larger station on foot through the light sprinkle which tapers to mist by the time he reaches the *plaça* in front of the station with the giant bullring to the east.

Agata has set out walking. He spots her yellow coat. She's already a block up Marques de Sotelo. He approximates her pace, which is moderate since she's towing her bag. The pavement is wet, but the air is tepid and feels warm and velvety compared to the plateau.

Luncheoners jam sidewalk cafés on peachy marble side-walks; lines await tables. Diners lean over enormous pans of steaming seafood paella heaped with prawns and mussels, and Dan is again sharply aware that he hasn't eaten since yesterday, and that wasn't much. Africans selling purses, sneakers, shirts and little folding wooden baskets have spread rows of blankets on the shiny sidewalks. In segments of mid-street parks, buskers play, sometimes audible over the roar of scooters. From some light-poles hang banners with somber black and white photos of fierce, determined women's faces underscored by slogans: *Non es non*, and *Respecte*.

The layout of the city is familiar to Dan. He stayed here with friends for several weeks.

He had drifted from his rented room on the hill near the domed Temppeliaukio church in Helsinki down the Baltics, slipping via nighttime rides hitched through Byelorussia, crossing the border in the back of a truck carrying a load of Mamont vodka but getting caught by a Politsiya patrol, released because he spoke beautiful Russian and the kindly old driver bribed the police with a few bottles of the vodka, a brand far above their pay-scale; then to Warsaw and hence southward, a pale northerner gravitating to warmth. As if to rebound from the cold, he labored for a time in a sauna-hot brick railyard warehouse in the Poblados Maritimos near Valencia's port, loading fifty-kilo cartons of green Montserrat tomatoes bound for Britain. The acidic stink of tomatoes thick in the building, the squelch of tomatoes underfoot; Dan didn't eat a tomato for two months after that job.

Agata crosses the Plaça de la Verge behind the cathedral and works her way back to a narrow, vertical hotel in a sidestreet off Carrer dels Serrans. The street is pedestrian-only and paved with red tile. Dan lounges in a doorway opposite. Through the glass front of the hotel, he sees her at the desk. He sees her at the elevator. He glimpses her in the hallway on the second floor and entering a room on the north side. The room has a small balcony.

Just beyond the hotel with its elegant gilt sign is a hostel labeled in blank script. The building is narrow, like the hotel. Dan enters the dusty lobby of the hostel. The clerk is Armenian. The clerk's Spanish is terrible, and his Catalan non-existent. Dan converses in Armenian, a language which formed part of his Master's thesis when he studied at Oxford. He asks if they have private rooms. They do. The hostel is largely empty, it being the off-season. He asks if there is a room available on the south side of the building toward the front, preferably on the second floor. It's a tiny space barely large enough to squeeze past the single bed with its thin cotton mattress, a dirty woven rug on the floor that sticks to his shoes, one steel chair; not exactly a parador, but it's adjacent to Agata's room, and it has a small balcony beside hers.

In the room, he washes out a pair of underwear and socks in the soup-bowl sized sink and hangs them to dry in the mildewed atmosphere. Toilet and shower are down the hall. The door to the room closes, but the deadbolt of the lock doesn't fit its socket. There is one overhead light fixture missing its shade.

He steps out to buy bread, salami, cheese and a bottle of wine at a bodega around a corner. Back in his room in the hostel, he eats and then pulls the chair out onto the balcony and sits, watching to see if Agata comes out of the hotel. But before long, owing to the food and lack of rest the previous thirty-six hours, he falls into hard, dreamless sleep. When he wakes, his legs are numb from the cold and the sharp-edged chair. Dark has descended into the network of slim, echoing streets in the old city. Laughter and distant music rise to him from the night.

Lights shine from the hotel room beside him, Agata's room, splashing out over its balcony which abuts his. Just then, he hears the scraping of the latches on the tall old doors with their rattling glass panes, and he stands and steps back into his room from his balcony just as she steps out onto hers. He hovers just inside the door of his room, listening.

She stretches her arms and shoulders in the cool air. She has perhaps been napping, as he was.

All that separates them is a thin cool garment of evening, the indirect echo of her from across the street. He hears her breathe, sigh. She goes back into her room. There are several minutes of small scrapes, things being softly moved, perhaps clothing and objects being pulled from a suitcase. He hears her murmur a chorus from a song.

He hears the tone of her voice, soft, a little girlish, approximating musical. He knows the lines she's singing. He mouths a phrase along with her.

Then her phone rings. He's leaning against the jamb of his balcony doors and, from around the corner, each word she says is clear. He hears, of course, only her side of the conversation.

"Hello."

"In Valencia. That was the plan."

"I wasn't feeling well yesterday."

"I don't know. Not far, I think."

"Like I said, I was feeling sick. I stopped in Cuenca to rest. I figured a small delay wouldn't hurt. Might be helpful to take it slowly, in fact."

"I called him. He was in the area. You knew that."

"I understand."

"I know."

"I know. Don't remind me."

"I'm sorry."

"Yes."

"Okay."

"Good night."

He hears her say something else, perhaps swear a little. A bed creaks as if under someone sitting or lying down. After a few minutes, the bed creaks again and she comes to her balcony and pushes her doors mostly closed, but he can still hear vague renditions of activities through the masonry wall, transmitted by the ancient wooden skeleton and vesicles of the interlaced buildings. Her shower runs for a long time. A few minutes after it stops, a hair dryer starts. There are some clunks, shuffling, soft sounds, as of clothing pulled onto her body. He clearly hears her say, apparently to herself, "Well I guess that's the way it goes," in English. The television comes on.

Dan turns away from the wall. She is too close, right there beyond the old stones. *Respecte.* He looks around the room. There is no television to turn on. He looks to his phone. He brings up the hostel's network, finds a music site, something to interfere with eavesdropping, Eurojazz and low Spanish chatter. It plays tinnily. At least sounds from the adjoining room are less obvious. He sits on his bed and opens one of the novels.

After a minute he sets down the book and assesses. He had been told that she would be heading east from Madrid. Valencia is east, but not far. Perhaps she is going further. There is apparently a plan for her travel. Her travel includes stops. However, she wasn't supposed to stop in Cuenca. She met with someone. Perhaps the comment he overheard referred to the man in the restaurant that Dan photographed and reported. If so, it possibly triangulates that she was talking to his handlers. This makes sense to some extent since she ostensibly works for them. But it seems to expose the fact that she knows that she's being watched.

Is Dan the only one watching her? The creeping sensation that he's being duped climbs through him. He fights this feeling.

But before long he notices that the television next door has turned off. Then he hears her room door closing and locking.

He spots her ahead of him in Serrans among the crowds out walking before dinner on the shining cobbles. She has switched back to the black coat and black boots. Her jeans, too, are black, and her scarf dark, either navy or purple. The only lighter color about her is the red hair, a fine shade of polished rust in the beckoning light spilling from stores and restaurants, that and a sparkle of little earrings as she turns to look at things left and right. She walks slowly. A few men turn to look at her, and a woman or two. Dan notices these looks.

Agata crosses the street, aims north toward the ancient stone gate and turns into Roteros, where are found some nicer eateries, and then into an Italian restaurant with bright windows and shining tables inside. The restaurant is already crowded, though it's barely nine. But as Dan strolls past on the sidewalk he sees an empty table behind the table at which Agata has seated herself. She is facing away from the window and into the dining room, a logical position to take for viewing the activity of a busy, warm restaurant.

On impulse, Dan turns and walks into the restaurant. He nods to the waiter at the door, aims a glance at the empty table behind Agata. The waiter says good evening and gestures welcome to the table. Dan slides into the chair facing away from Agata, as if he is more interested in watching traffic passing in the street while he eats.

He is sitting less than a meter from her. They are back to back. He can see a reflection of her back in the window. She has taken off her coat. She is wearing a thin sweater and still has her scarf on. She studies the menu.

Dan examines the menu also, coat still on, poised on his chair as if reconsidering this reckless maneuver. But then he sits back and breathes deeply. She would only recognize him if she looked straight at his face and if she remembered him from the moment they brushed past each other in her apartment foyer, both unlikely. He removes his coat and orders bottled water and wine.

They eat their salads. Her Spanish, when she speaks to the waiter, is mediocre: adequate, even comfortable, but clumsy. She smiles at something the waiter says. Her upper teeth angle slightly back, he notices in her reflection. Then her phone buzzes and she slides it out of her purse. As in the hotel, Dan hears her side.

"I can't talk now."

"I'll tell you later."

"Nothing's wrong, I just can't talk. I'm eating."

"OK."

The waiter brings their dinners, both at the same time. "That smells good," Agata says to the waiter. He is solicitous to her and brings her more bread and water, pours her wine for her. Perhaps because Dan is nervous-looking, the waiter is more diffident with him. When the waiter asks if the meal is satisfactory, Dan only nods. When the waiter asks if Dan would like to see the dessert menu, he says no thank you in Greek for some reason, but the gist is received.

Agata pulls a paperback from her bag and reads while she sips wine and slowly twirls pasta. Reading in restaurants is a habit Dan has long cherished. He turns just enough to glimpse the spine of the book, a cheap British Penguin edition, when she sets it down to tear bread: Bronte's *Agnes Grey*.

Dan finishes his wine. He signals for the check. He is so close to her he can her hear chew, even possibly smell her shampoo, her skin. His posture in his chair is somewhere between flight and settlement, torn, the tension frozen in his legs and back of being just about to stand, but not standing. The discomfort of watching this woman, listening to her, perusing and pursuing her, is only numbed by the presumption that she is a criminal, that she is associated with people who steal things. Perhaps she participates in that. It's difficult for Dan to reconcile the angles.

When Agata stands to leave, she bumps Dan's back slightly and he hears her say excuse me. The waiter helps her with her coat and then she leaves. Dan hands the waiter some bills and sets off with urgency. He would not be able to say whether he is more concerned about seeing everywhere she goes or simply remaining close to her.

Back in his room he hears her checking the locks on her shutters for the night. He texts his handlers: "A.S. in Valencia alone. No contacts."

He sleeps through much of the night, mild sequences of dreams in their proper periods, gentle and regenerative, though scant.

CHAPTER 11

VALENCIA
6 November, Monday

He wakes long before light. Dan takes a walk. All is silent in the streets of Valencia save a few sleepy scooters and very early delivery vans. He receives four hundred Euros from a bank machine on the street just around the corner off Plaça de la Mare de Deu. Nearby, a shiny new Vespa stands in the spilling light of an all-night bodega. He pauses to admire it, and thinks of his daughter Genevieve riding one like it around Paris. This is a compelling image for him. He squeezes the wallet in his pocket, which thickens daily.

It's too early for coffee in a café, so he takes a vague milky caffeine drink from a rattling cooler in the bodega. To pay, he must wake the clerk, who sleeps in a back room.

He has just turned the corner into the street of his hostel and Agata's hotel when he sees her climbing into a taxi. She is wearing the yellow coat. The driver is loading her silver suitcase into the car's trunk. She glances around from the back seat. The car slips away up the pre-dawn street in the direction of Serrans.

Dan runs into Agata's hotel and says to the desk clerk in Catalan, "My friend Agata Svendson had to leave before I had a chance to talk to her. Where is she going?"

Startled, the desk clerk says, "To the airport." Then she looks at Dan in perplexity and the chagrin of revealing unwarranted gossip.

Dan comes back out onto the street just as another taxi draws up, perhaps a second taxi responding hopefully to the call for Agata's taxi, perhaps just serendipitous, an odd occurrence since this is a pedestrian avenue and taxis would usually only come here on order. His decision must be quick. He climbs into the taxi. The driver says, "Airport?"

Traffic is still light. The driver mentions that there is an accident on the V-30 which is slowing access to the A-3. He circles down to Carre de Quart and around the doubled Torre, holed by Napoleon's cannons and purpled by the promise of sunrise, under the dark sweep of the botanic gardens to green-belt-divided Catolic. They cross the bridge of Glories Valencianes over the old, dry riverbed park with stray early cyclists and joggers and dog walkers below on the shadowy paths.

Dan's satchel is in his room. On his person, he has the fake passport and his wallet with his accumulated cash and debit card and an expired driver's license. He has the phone that they gave him. He has lost the phone he bought for himself, his binoculars, journals, books and all his spare clothing. He wears his cotton jacket over his slept-in sweater and a pair of jeans.

There is, of course, no sign of Agata's taxi. She is at least five minutes ahead, and from here it's all freeways with burgeoning rush hour traffic in a multitude of directions, onramps clogged in the dark, unending streams of headlights. Or Agata's driver may have taken another route, down to Avenida del Cid and up to the A-3. Logically, she must be going to the departures terminal.

In the airport, Dan rushes to the security area. Swelling lines of people head for early flights. Agata is not in the queues, nor does he see her in the concourses beyond. He circles back to the rows of check-in counters and jogs along them all the way to the car rental area, scanning left and right. Travelers foam and swirl around him. He spins. Then the sea retreats and there she is walking from the right with her suitcase, probably from the restrooms, toward the check-in counters. She passes fifty steps from him. For a moment, there is only open space between them, and she glances his way. Her eyes seem to pass over him. Her expression relaxes. Perhaps the bathroom visit was an urgency. She seems to be searching for the correct row of counters.

She bypasses the line at an airline counter and goes to an automated check-in kiosk. She slides her passport through the scanner, taps the screen. Dan watches from a distance now, from behind crowds of families with mountains of luggage, a glut of yawning British college students with peach-soft, hungover faces, a cluster of athletic but exhausted men, probably some sort of team, in matching polo shirts.

His way forward now is unclear. That is, until she steps away from her machine and starts toward the security line. He slides quickly along the row of banded barrier to the kiosks and to the machine she just used. The kiosk dispensed her boarding pass, a receipt and an itinerary card. Agata took the boarding pass and receipt but left the itinerary card in the slot.

Dan takes the card. She has purchased a two-leg ticket. She is going to Nice this morning on the 7:15 flight and on to Rome the next morning. A minute ago, his enterprise had faced its conclusion. He now stands in the noise and light of the departures terminal gazing down at the little manila card and wondering at this luck, and, because he's not stupid, if such a coincidence could be luck.

He takes the phone from his pocket. He texts: "A.S. flying out of Valencia." He considers getting something to eat while waiting for a response. But pausing for permission may eliminate opportunity. So, he steps to the ticket counter.

He asks for a seat on the 7:15 to Nice, one way. The agent asks him if he has baggage to check, and then takes his passport and slides it through the scanner. Dan glances to the doors of the terminal, a distance of a few dozen meters from the counter. He may be able to run and melt into the crowds, if he needs to. He looks back at the agent. The agent rocks on his feet looking at the screen. Dan watches his face, which alters from boredom to vague perplexity. He says, "Let me try it this way," and he keys in the passport number. They wait again, and then he looks up brighter. "That time it worked," he shrugs.

Dan pays with cash. He takes his boarding pass and goes to the security line. There his passport is scanned again, and it seems to clog the system. But with a retry the machine beeps and the guard waves Dan through. Guards with assault rifles stand beyond, chatting. Dan steps through the portal and collects his belongings. A phalanx of cameras fan down from the low ceilings and Dan glances up as he passes under them. Just then his phone vibrates. The text says, "Follow."

Dan searches for credit card phones in the concourse. If he can reach the hostel, he can explain that he left his bag in his room and ask if they will hold it for a few days. He has old friends in Valencia. Maybe someone can pick it up for him. But before he can do anything, the airline announces his flight.

The 737 is mostly full. Agata sits toward the front. She looks down into her riveted purse as Dan passes in the aisle. Pre-flight announcements rattle through, English attractively-dressed in Irish tones, after which an approximation in Spanish and a few perfunctory words in Italian. Dan sends a final text: "A.S. to Nice."

CHAPTER 12

NICE

6 November, Monday

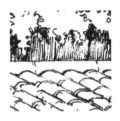

The plane descends to the airport angled on its broad spit of land southwest of the city. Sunlight on the diamond sea causes passengers to slap down window shades as the plane circles, but Dan watches the geography unfold out his window.

Dan exits the terminal just as Agata reaches the taxi queue. He catches a single word, Negresco, as she speaks to the driver. This simplifies the task of tailing her into the city. Dan's taxi pulls to a stop just off Promenade des Anglais as Agata is mounting the timeworn marble steps into the Hotel Negresco. Under its glass-arch canopy, a red-suited bellman whisks open the door. Dan follows at a distance, hands in pockets, nodding to the bellman.

Agata checks in and trundles to the elevator. Left with nothing to do, Dan sinks into a scooped leather armchair. Off the lobby to one side, a gift shop; on the other, the hotel restaurant. In the gift shop, he peruses books. He selects a copy of the Pléiade edition of Giono's *Horseman on the Roof* in a slim format. Purchase completed, he slips it into the pocket of his canvas jacket.

In the lobby, he sits in the armchair again. The elevators open onto a niche around the corner from the desk, and the stairs descend into the same area. He will see Agata when she comes down, unless by taking a back stairway she eludes him, which she could do at any time, although she has shown no inclination to elude anyone. He reads for a while, drifts. In the book's introduction, an old quote from Giono that he remembers from a previous read: *Civilization tries to persuade us we are going towards something, a distant goal. We have forgotten that our only goal is to live, to live each and every day, and that if we live each and every day, our true goal is achieved.* Dan reaches for his notebook but is reminded of the loss of his satchel.

In the lobby, a little girl tugs at her mother's hand. The mother engages in conversation with others, two men and an older woman, all apparently family judging by the cut of face and expressions and quality of hair. The girl, perhaps six or seven years old, dances, gapes about. She sees Dan. She slowly disentangles her fingers from her mother's. Unnoticed by family, she approaches Dan. She stands nearby for a moment looking at him, evidently sizing him up. Then she lifts and displays a small item in her hand. In French, she says, "I found this, but my Mom won't let me keep it." She shakes the item gently at Dan and then opens her fingers to allow him to see a small stuffed animal. Worn and scuffed, it may have been intended to resemble a squirrel, or a rabbit.

"My Mom says it's dirty. I found it out there." The girl points to the front doors of the hotel, suggesting the greater world of Nice or France.

"It's very nice."

She looks at it sideways. Then she looks back at him. Her face, her eyes and the way she tilts her gaze at him, evaluating, thinking things through, duplicates his daughters. Sitting in the lobby of the old hotel in sight of the famous Baccarat chandelier, Dan sees them in this girl's face.

"Will you keep it? For me? Until we come back? My Mom says I can't." The girl looks at him closely. Her eyes are satin steel, a judge's gaze. "I trust you," she says.

Dan looks over at the family. They remain engaged. There seems some discord, some matter of logistics or budget or fatigue.

"Okay, I will keep it," he says to the girl. She hands him the stuffed animal carefully, watching what he does with it. Dan smiles. He studies it closely for a moment. Its shape, the creature it represents, remains indefinite. It has apparently been run over in a road several times, washed by rains, perhaps animal-chewed. He tucks it into the pocket of his jacket opposite the copy of Giono.

The girl smiles. She says, "We have to go visit my grandparents. Then we're coming back. My Dad was supposed to get a car but he forgot." Dan smiles into her little face. He again looks up at the family. He can see the mother only in profile, her managerial expression perhaps the future of the daughter's. The little girl turns and dashes back to the group as they exit the Negresco.

Not long after they have left, Agata comes quickly down carpeted stairs. She wears slim almond slacks, a tight green shirt, low pale shoes. She carries her small black purse. She stops at the concierge desk to ask a question. The concierge points upstreet. He offers a brochure which she declines. She exits the hotel and walks up Rue de Rivoli.

Two blocks up, a scooter rental shop fronts the boulevard. Red scooters, Piaggio 50 CC models, lean on their kickstands in a row along the chipped granite curb. Printed banners blaze invitations. Agata enters the shop and talks to a man for several minutes. He wears blade-like sunglasses even indoors. They exit and he pulls a scooter off its kickstand for her. He starts it. He turns it off. They go back inside. From across the street, Dan sees the two of them at the counter, the man talking and slicking back his hair, she signing papers.

Dan crosses and stands in the doorway of a café adjacent to the scooter rental shop. He is around a corner, but he hears Agata

65

say to the shop owner as she steps outside, "I'll be back in fifteen minutes." He watches as she walks up Rue de Rivoli. He makes a quick calculation. He goes to the scooter shop and tells the man, standing looking after Agata, that he wants to rent a scooter.

The process takes several minutes. There is a form to fill out. The man sizes Dan up and says, "You need something taller." He goes into the repair shop in the back and returns a few minutes later wheeling a white Yamaha. It is slightly larger than the Piaggios lined up along the street. On the patio of the shop, the man starts the machine, revs it a little.

Back inside, he asks for Dan's driver's license. Dan in fact still has his Canadian driver's license in his wallet, although it expired five years earlier. He shows it to the man, with his finger partially covering.

"I need to make a copy," the man says.

Dan hands it to him, asking at the same time if the weather is slated to remain good. The man chats as he makes a copy of the license. He hands it back to Dan without looking at it, staples the copy to the form. Dan pays the deposit and daily rental fee in cash. Dan circles the block on the scooter. He waits upstreet some distance for Agata to return. A nearby kiosk sells tourist items. Dan steps off the bike and purchases a six-Euro pair of sunglasses, round with silvered lenses and wire frames. He also purchases a fifteen-Euro wristwatch with a sailboat on its blue face. As he steps away from the kiosk he sees Agata returning from the direction of the hotel. She carries nothing. She has put on her large oval sunglasses and tied an ivory bandanna around her hair.

She dons her open-faced helmet over the bandanna and adjusts the chin strap, fixes her sunglasses. The scooter rental man starts the bike again and shows her a few things, the throttle, the brakes, the turn signals. Agata nods quickly. She has ridden scooters before, apparently, but when she sets off, she is wobbly and slow. Dan watches until she reaches the end of the block and then starts slowly after her.

Agata pulls into the eastbound lane of Anglais and proceeds along the seafront past modernistic pergolas and thick, low palms. Crowds of strollers meander seaside walkways. On the beach, a few swim-suited souls lay out blankets and beach chairs in November sunshine.

Traffic heaves around the port. Agata proceeds in steps, slowing frequently to let trucks maneuver past. Dan lingers far behind. Although disguised by helmet and glasses, if she looks in her mirrors frequently and closely she may notice the same bike always there. But she seems to concentrate more on obstacles ahead.

Once past the great old walls of the citadel darkly shadowing the road, she slows in Villefranche with its fish stalls and flower markets and thronged cafés, and then along the beach promenade. At one point, when Agata brakes for a clot of pedestrians, Dan inadvertently catches up with her. At this range, he sees her face as she turns her head right and left, looking over the beach, nodding to passersby. She is smiling and bright. He sees her laugh.

Watching another person closely, a sensation of intimacy naturally develops. For several days, Dan has watched little else than this woman, her shape ahead of him, her postures and gestures, her actions, brief but hard-sought glimpses of her face. She is familiar to him now, a constant. The separation between them stretches and contracts but remains elastic. His thoughts and moods undulate with her movements. Her shadow has become an umbrella. The wary notion of her proposed connection to criminality fades a little each day, each new episode of trailing.

Agata's speed increases as she circles Saint-Jean-Cap-Ferrat, and her posture on the machine improves. The breeze off the water has stiffened. Whitecaps clatter. Several sailboats exit the marina at Beaulieu-sur-Mer angling south toward open sea, crews on decks unstrapping mainsails and shaking out genoas.

Agata parks near some street stalls and asks a man in an art booth for directions. Dan waits a half-block behind. Astride his idling scooter, his hands rest in his jacket pockets. He feels the book in one pocket and the stuffed animal in the other.

Back on her scooter, Agata tucks into the winding road which ascends the hills from the little harbor. Dan follows at a distance. Ubiquitous limestone walls slide past draping cataracts of yellow and purple anemones. His scooter labors with the climb. He opens the throttle full, but to negligible effect. She will reach the Moyenne Corniche ahead of him and he does not want to miss which direction she turns.

But when he rounds the last curve she is waiting at the junction as a line of cars passes before pulling onto the road heading east. The highway is traffic-laden. It swerves and widens into a divided road, passes through short tunnels. Agata hunches over the handlebars, keeping strictly to the right shoulder. Hordes of traffic, including many other scooters, roar past her. But she proceeds stubbornly uphill, and before long emerges into the cramped cluster of commercialism near the medieval village of Èze humped and spilling over its cactus-lined ridge above the vast golden platter of shining sea.

Agata parks in a row of motorbikes at the upper edge of a large carpark and stows her helmet. She removes the bandanna and fluffs her hair. She flutters her shirt away from her body to dry it. Dan coasts slowly into the carpark behind her with his jacket unzipped and flapping as Agata begins the pedestrian route into the old town.

Tourists swarm Èze. They meander in chattering clouds past glinting galleries and flowery perfumeries under a choppy sea of slate-tiled roofs, a tender quaintness. Although a town of charcoal and cinder-white, the blue ache of the Mediterranean rises and fills the eye, shattering into a thousand colors off every edge, every window box and tossing cluster of crocus and periwinkle.

Wending behind, Dan loses Agata a few times in the crowds, but the town is narrow and scant.

Agata leans on a stone parapet overlooking the russet hill-sides and the ocean. She is only there a minute when a man comes up and stands beside her. On the far side of the little square behind them, Dan slowly slips out his company phone. He opens the camera and zooms. Agata and the man are chatting with familiarity. He is about her height. When he turns toward her, Dan sees that it is the same man she met at the restaurant in Cuenca. His hair is silver. His black jacket is elegant. Agata smiles at him several times.

Before long, they turn to each other and share a quick, friendly hug. They part. The man walks past Dan to a set of narrow steps ascending between buildings. Dan is still holding his phone aloft, and as the man passes he gets a shot of his shoulder and face, his sharp features, his small tortoiseshell sunglasses. He disappears up the steps.

Agata steers back down the main avenue toward the bottom of the town, looping through throngs, smiling and stepping around buskers and jugglers, bypassing Fragonard and its network of shopping lanes. She mounts her scooter and has left the village before he has started his bike. He spots her turning west onto the Corniche, and with a roar he powers his scooter up and over the hump, weightless and sun-splashed, scented with heat and flowers, swerving through traffic. Agata's scooter is a half-kilometer ahead. She descends, elbows out, along the tight shoulder of the ancient Roman highway.

She threads and weaves on her scooter, her waist having learned in the past few hours to flex in accord with the trajectory and weight of the little machine, expertly. Where earlier in the day Dan was obliged to stall and hang back, now he struggles to keep up, to keep her in sight as they move back down into Nice through dawdling afternoon traffic in the roundabouts.

He waits again up the street, in a cluster of parked motorbikes in front of a café, while Agata returns her scooter at the shop.

Then Dan returns his scooter. The man in slashing sunglasses gives him a puzzled look as he comes in. "I noticed after you'd left that your driver's license has expired," he says. Dan affects a perplexed expression.

He returns to the Negresco, sits at a curve of the bar where he can view the lobby and orders a gin and bitters cocktail. In his jacket pockets, he feels the book on one side and the stuffed animal on the other. He reads a few dozen pages of Giono. The little girl and her family are not in evidence.

An hour passes. Dan has a second cocktail since they are well-suited to the warm afternoon. Then he goes to the front desk of the hotel and asks a woman there to ring Agata Svendson's room. He takes the call at a house phone in a nearby niche. After several rings, she answers. "Hello," she says. "I beg your pardon. I must have the wrong room," Dan says. "That's okay," she says and laughs softly. He stands at the phone for several minutes. They have spoken to each other. They may never speak again. He considers this, remembering how it felt.

He sits in a chair in the far corner of the lobby, screened behind potted palms, reading. He puts the half-finished book into his jacket pocket. He removes the stuffed animal from the other. His mission was to keep it for the little girl while she was out for the day. Nothing had been said about the plan for returning it, and perhaps such restoration was not implied.

Dan turns and installs the stuffed animal behind the rim of a potted fern, its remnant of face with one beaded eye peeking out between fronds. The animal looks cheerful. The little girl may spot it there, waiting for her, before the cleaning staff, if she is sharp-eyed, if she comes again into this area of the lobby, if her family is still in this hotel, if she really cared about this fragment of linen and lint. But Dan's expression is of someone who doubts he is worthy of trust.

Agata comes through the lobby. She wears the black jeans, a grey knit jacket, a thin scarf. She exits the hotel, crosses Promenade des Anglais and goes for a stroll. The sun has set toward Spain; the evening has cooled dramatically. She descends to the pebbly beach and to the edge of the water. For several minutes she stands still, gazing out over the sea. The afternoon's wind has died completely, and vast towers of cumulus have coiled up over the ocean, billowing crests still glowing over cloaked midriffs.

She stands alone on the beach, and Dan stands alone on the promenade above and behind her. Then she lifts her arms and stretches them out to the sea, to the approximate place the sun last occupied, melting aubergine across the black water. She stands like this for a minute. Her form is dark against the pewter gravel beach and the slight foam of negligible surf in the stones.

Later, Dan texts, "A.S. in Nice. No contacts observed." This lie is intended as a test which might coax additional facts to the surface. Either his handlers know who Agata is meeting, or they don't. Their response may clarify. But he falls asleep in his modest hotel a block from the Negresco having received no reply.

CHAPTER 13

IN FLIGHT
7 November, Tuesday

In the morning there is still no response.

Their flight aims for Rome's old Ciampino just south of the city, not gigantic Fiumicino out by the coast. Agata's itinerary stated that she was flying one way to Rome. But she might have a continuing ticket on another airline, or she may buy one in Rome. The indication from his handlers had been that she had eastern connections. She might be hopping to Bratislava, Bucharest or Budapest on this airline, or further if on another. Either way, if she transfers to another plane, she will route through the connections concourse and it will be difficult to discern where she is going since, to the best of his recollection, there are security layers in place between concourses now. Consequently, the end of his path may be an airport in Rome.

But if she stops in Rome, a second issue is presented. If she takes a taxi into the city, it will be difficult to track her given the traffic and scale of the place. If she takes a bus, it will be awkward to wait in line for the same bus, get on behind her and get off at her destination all without her noticing him. She might have already observed him in the restaurant in Valencia, or at the airport, or in the crowds of Èze. Seeing the same person again would cause anyone a doubletake.

However, she might take the train. A Trenitalia line from Ciampino drops into Termini.

Dan considers all angles as the plane descends over Corsica. Below, lines of breakers scrape white against the western shores of the island. A line of thunderheads shuffled up overnight from the general direction of Algeria, but the morning has cleared. The citadel, the bay and harbor at Salvi stand out, including details of the marina. Dan sailed a boat into this harbor once, not long after the last time he had seen his wife Angelique in person.

The boat's owner, a wealthy brewer from Luxembourg, succumbed to seasickness partway across the Ligurian in the middle of the night and sank moaning into a berth below.

Dan stalked the deck alone in the spray through the night, sea and sky impenetrable save for the distant lights of a few anchovy and seabream boats venturing back toward La Spezia through snarly squalls, shaking off the anticipated despair of losing touch with his second daughter, occasionally checking the radar. At dawn, he singlehanded the 60-foot sloop into Salvi harbor.

He spent ten days meandering little villages along the granite epaulets of Corsica, sitting with locals in the shade of chestnuts through the hammering heights of the days, sipping glove-soft wines and conversing, absorbing phrases and pronunciations, hitching rides with farmers in old Toyota pickups loaded with salt-rimed cheeses and crocks of honey, sleeping on the yacht through soft halyard-pinging nights in the marina under the citadel with the distant throb of Euro-trance from the clubs along Rue Georges Clemenceau.

He did what he could to survive the comments with which Angelique had left him:

"It might be best if you didn't visit again. It's too hard on Genevieve."

74

Dan had stood in the doorway of Angelique's apartment in Paris.
"She lost her sister," he said. "She shouldn't lose her father, too."
"It's too late for that," Angelique had said.

At Ciampino, Agata queues for the train into the city.

Boarded, she is somewhere in the forward half of the train. Dan stands twice but cannot see her. When they reach Termini, he hurries out and spots her already far down the platform and entering the main concourse. He trails her threading course among the shops and kiosks and turmoil of Termini.

Agata bypasses the taxi queues and crosses Via Giovanni Giolitti. Dan follows into wan November sunshine and the blare of Rome. Few pedestrians wait for signals or even pause for legions of onracing scooters. It is almost noon on a late-autumn Tuesday. A bronze and emotive sky hangs above. A woman with an unusually large nose ring approaches him in the piazza with a petition, something to do with curing or saving, *sanare* or *salvare*, Dan doesn't quite catch over the roar of traffic. Two blocks ahead, Agata is turning the corner onto Via Cavour.

He tracks Agata past ethnic restaurants, clothing shops, street peddlers and money changers down the long blocks, keeping his now customary distance. Among midday crowds, her coppery hair, the shape of her back seen from a distance, her carriage and gait have become familiar, reassuring.

She continues on foot westward downhill on Viminale, cuts north briefly on Quatro Fontane and then cross-town again on Nazionale, the slow rolling passage along the Quirinale toward the Forum, the wedding cake rising in the distance ahead, the crag of the Coliseum to the left over tiled rooftops. Hands in pockets, Dan trundles along a few blocks behind.

Morning scooter clamor ululates along the boulevard. Rooftop gardens above wear their trussed autumn greys.

Thousands of starlings blacken the trees in the park at Villa Aldobrandini cacophonously; they rise in swirling clouds when a dog runs through. Agata's suitcase clips along over the broad stones, and he hears it occasionally during lulls in traffic. She walks casually, unhurried by clock or weather. Cirrus over the ancient brick and marble city rips in the breeze like raw silk across the sun and offers only a nonchalant gesture of overcast. She's wearing the black coat this morning and a pastel blue scarf he doesn't recognize, the sleek black jeans and her running shoes.

She skirts the two domed churches, old favorites of Dan's, opposite Trajan's Column, then crosses Corso at the Palace of Domitian and proceeds to a hotel a couple blocks up the avenue. The hotel is a boutique and faces directly onto Corso. Passing on the sidewalk, Dan sees Agata at the reception desk in the slight, golden lobby.

The building is too intimate for him to stay there also, and there are no sidewalk cafés in this stretch of Corso offering advantage points from which to watch. There is, however, a cluster of hotels in the area, and one in particular seems obvious, a polished edifice directly across Corso with corner-room balconies facing the street.

The price for one of these rooms is cringe-worthy, but Dan takes it, and prepays for a night. Like the parador, it is in fact one of the nicer hotel rooms he has ever occupied. When he traveled with Angelique they tended to economize, and when he traveled with the Canadian national sailing team and later on CSIS business, hotels were government-stipulated. He roams the suite, sits on the bed, pats the comforter. There are chocolates, flowers, fruit in a bowl, bottles of spring water. The furniture is reproduction antique and very soft, the carpet thick and snowy. He takes a chair carefully onto the balcony along with a cup of tea and sits in the sun which is just beginning to cross the face of the building.

Most of the tall windows on the hotel across the street have their drapes pulled. In an open window, he sees a housekeeper cleaning. In another he sees a man sitting at a desk writing. Down the street, a car attempting to parallel park scrapes its fender hard on a granite post, and the driver climbs out to inspect; a passerby stops to commiserate. The car blocks traffic and horns sound.

Then Dan sees Agata emerge from her hotel. She wears multi-colored tights, a gunmetal running jacket, her running shoes, a cap and sunglasses. She stands against the wall stretching her legs one at a time by hooking the instep of a foot in her hand and pulling upward, then reversing. She stretches her calves by placing her palms against the wall and reaching each foot backward. Then she bounces on her toes, full of energy, and sets off at a brisk run. He sees her thread the traffic across Corso at Piazza Venetia and head in the direction of the Coliseum, her long colorful legs moving quickly, visible until she turns the corner below mighty Vittorio Emanuele.

As in Madrid, he cannot follow, so he sits back to wait. Going for a run would be a method for her to elude him to meet someone, but that assumes she knows he is tracking her, and he must stick with the only workable assumption, which is that she doesn't know he's there.

Dan selects an orange from the bowl. He removes his shoes and walks back and forth on the carpet a few times. He looks in the minibar, admires the notion of a Bombay and tonic, but returns to the balcony with a mineral water. It is cool out, so he wears his jacket.

Sitting in the sunshine with the gentle din of Via del Corso drifting up, eating orange slices and sipping Norwegian bottled water, he takes his money from his wallet. He has roughly four thousand Euros in cash from the combined inaugural payment and accumulated per diems. This is after he paid several hundred to his landlady in Madrid to catch up on back rent for his garret room and replaced his clothing and added sundries. A week has elapsed. They said the task would consume two weeks. Could he make it last possibly three? Dan would like to stretch it as much as possible, of course. Then there is the promise of an additional payment at the conclusion. With the amassed sum, he should be able to help Genevieve, buy her a nice new scooter, as he had been considering, a Vespa or Aprilia or whatever is cool in Paris that year, or even help make the down payment on whatever she wants, a business or a house. He no longer knows what his daughter wants. Not that she was ever transparent with him, or anyone.

Via del Corso pulses below him, with its mobs of tourists loudly wending toward Fontana di Trevi, the Spanish Steps and Piazza del Popolo at the far end, if they're feeling ambitious. Waves of scooters bear scowly Romans in heavy-rimmed eyeglasses and skinny pants, beeping taxis and Smart cars also in the mix.

He had last seen Genevieve five years earlier, on a visit to Chamonix. At the time, he had been living in Copenhagen, an early waypoint before Helsinki, Mannheim, Glasgow, Marrakech, Toulouse, farmlands along the valleys of the Rhine, the Rhone, the Po, the Danube, the Douro, the Vistula, stints on Cyprus and Corfu, fishing boats from Porto to Izmir, before stopping in Madrid. Along the way, he worked as migrant laborer, freelance translator, longshore hauler, itinerant tutor, anywhere he could find informal work and a room to sleep in, usually with the assistance and behest of people he met as he moved, people he ran into and befriended and who came to admire and protect him, always within some manageable Schengen radius of Paris.

If he'd wanted to disappear, he might have slipped south into Tunis or Cairo without excessive passport scrutiny, and from there made his way to Nairobi or Harare and started a new life. This man had the talent and guile to successfully self-exile.

But somewhere between all that happened behind and a shack somewhere forward, maybe along some palm-lined beach in Madagascar, lay the subtle, forceful seduction of Europe. He could not pull away.

There had been conversations with Angelique scattered along, a few per year, always with her only, not with Genevieve who, according to Angelique, didn't hate her father but sank into impenetrable sadness whenever she spoke with him. On the occasions he called the number he had for her, Genevieve never answered. He asked Angelique not to isolate him. He sent letters to his daughter, care of Angelique, but received nothing in return except one time a postcard from the Great Wall with a few wish-you-were-here lines and a smiley face.

He sent her little gifts at Christmas and on her birthday, which was also in late December, things that struck him as being appropriate for a girl her age, which shot him through with the sorrow of not knowing his daughter, the topography of her delights and tragedies and daily life, the person she had become. He tended to think of her as a baby, a toddler, the heft and smell of her in his arms. But if she sent thank-you notes for the gifts, he did not receive them, possibly because he was so often on the move.

He glances at the time on his watch. If Agata is a strong, aggressive runner, as every indication suggests, she won't return for another fifteen or twenty minutes. He keys Angelique's number, which he knows by heart, up to the last digit into the hotel phone and then pauses for a full minute. She often doesn't answer or return his calls. Her silences club and defeat him.

Each time he tries her and receives nothing, a ragged injury to his soul deepens and widens. He shakes his head at dull-witted perseverance.

He dials the final digit of her number. Her phone rings twice. She answers.

"Hello?"

"Hi," he says.

"Dan. Hello. Where are you calling from?"

"Rome. I lost my other phone."

"I got your message. I was going to call this weekend. Are you okay? You sound." Angelique pauses.

"How do I sound?"

"You sound good. I just wanted to make sure."

"I'm good."

"Good."

"You?"

"I'm good too."

"I'm working now."

"Yes, you mentioned that. Where are you in Rome?"

"You remember that place we stayed one time over near the Pantheon? The place where the roof leaked when it rained? Not far from there."

Angelique asks, "What sort of work are you doing?"

"Just some research for some people."

"Is it safe? Research. When you use that tone, it sounds like you're doing something dangerous."

"Nothing dangerous. I just don't feel like going into the details. It's boring."

"Very vague. I'm worried. With you, vague means you don't

80

want to talk about it, and if you don't want to talk, it means you're ashamed or scared."

Dan cannot or does not wish to evade this point. Instead, he says, "Are you still exercising a lot?"

"Oh yes," she says reassuringly. "I'm doing a triathlon in Reykjavik in a few months. I started CrossFit. Do you know what that is?"

"No," says Dan.

"It's a program. Very hard."

"What for?"

"It's hard."

"What for?"

"Hard is good," she says. "Don't be such a baby."

"Don't hurt yourself," Dan says. "We're not kids anymore." This brings silence again. After a while, he says, "How's Gennie?"

"She's fine. She's working at a theater. She's an assistant stage manager three nights a week, so it doesn't interfere with her classes at École Normale Supérieure. She made the dean's list again last quarter. Her boyfriend got her the job. He's something of a well-known actor here, in certain circles. At least I think he's a he. He has sideburns. Jules Free. That's his name. He's nice. Very artsy and – alternative, I guess is the best term. He's older. I think he's about thirty. But you know Genevieve. She's a vegan now, but it hasn't hurt her. At least Jules bathes regularly and dresses to the nines, unlike the last one."

"I would like to see you and Gennie," Dan ventures.

Angelique says, "I would like to see you, too."

Dan pauses, surprised. "When I'm done here. Shouldn't be

long. I'll have some time. As if I have anything but time."

She laughs a little.

He continues, wistfully. "Why did we ever break up?" At that moment, he's not asking specifically or rhetorically.

She backs away, falls into a single tone. "If I remember correctly, because you were fucking a co-worker girl who worked for you in Montreal, and even when I'd more or less gotten past that, you'd become so sad and distant and cold, I couldn't imagine spending another day in the house with you, much less the rest of my life. And then Adrienne, and things went downhill."

Dan retains the dignity to stay silent. His silence speaks for both. The line remains quiet for a few moments.

Then Angelique says, "The point is, please don't try to suggest that we made a mistake. No mistake has been made. We are where we are. We don't have to like it. But I would still like to see you. And Genevieve has asked about you several times recently. She even asked if I had an address or number for you. I gave her the number that you gave me. I'm surprised she hasn't called you yet. She's changed, Dan. Grown. I get the sense she wants her father back in her life, and I think that's a good thing now."

Angelique clears her throat, as if composing herself, then continues.

"I have to be up front with you, Dan. I'd also like to move forward with getting a divorce. I might want to get married again sometime. My lawyer says you wouldn't have to do anything but sign the papers. Your status doesn't matter. It has to be notarized, but my lawyer says he can take care of that."

"Are you seeing someone at that level?" Dan asks in a voice resembling an interviewer. "He's not the personal trainer, right?"

"Yes, maybe, and no, not the trainer. His name is Gregor. He's Hungarian but has lived in France for decades. He has some television stations. A magazine. His Paris house is in the 8th. Staff of four, formal gardens, 18th-century library. He also has a big place, an old castle, along the Vaud near Gstaad where we go skiing. He's a little old-fashioned. His grandmother was a countess a hundred years ago, and his business associates call him count. Traditional Catholic family, the apostolic royalty and all that. That's why the divorce. Besides, you and I have just been drifting along for seven years avoiding reality."

Dan says nothing.

After a minute, Angelique asks in a lilt resembling cheerfulness, "Are you seeing anyone?" Her voice over the phone has taken on a little shakiness, a splash more emotion.

"Yes," Dan says.

"What's her name?"

"Agata," he says.

"Is she good to you?"

"Of course," Dan says.

"Well, maybe things are moving along then."

After they conclude and hang up, he goes inside, dumps out his cold tea, runs a hot shower in the long glass stall and remains under the tropical torrent for several minutes. He is standing at the window in the thick bathrobe found in the closet when he sees Agata come back into her hotel walking with a loose, stretchy, post-run stride.

Dan also sees a man walk by her hotel just after she enters. The man slows and looks through the glass doors, as if trying to catch a glimpse of her. The man wears a black coat. He has a black mustache. He is smoking. He looks like any one of millions of other men. But he seems vaguely familiar to Dan, as if they've met somewhere in the past, that little flutter of déjà vu that comes with feeling one should recognize something that one doesn't.

CHAPTER 14

ROME
7 November, Tuesday

After dark, Agata emerges and walks north on Corso. She carries nothing but her small purse, casually. She turns left on Via del Pié de Marmo and passes the Collegio Romano with its lounging hordes of students in the parking lot opposite the wall embedded with imperial Corinthian columns. Agata enters Santa Maria Sopra Minerva.

Dan crosses the piazza with its elephant and obelisk and leans against a low wall beside the Pantheon to wait for her. She comes out of the church a few minutes later, gives some change to a beggar on the steps and continues downhill beside the Pantheon and the gelato shops.

The evening is downy. The breeze has stopped. Starlings storm the sky over the city. The *passeggiata* has started early, robust and colorful. Around the fountain facing the Pantheon, jugglers and musicians vie for attention and coins. Jammed cafés ring the piazza.

Agata threads into the nearly-empty Pantheon. Dan slips between the massive columns after her and stands in the portal. Agata slowly circles the vast space, her face uptilted to the dome and the oculus. A small group of pigeons clusters in the center of the floor, cooing in the gloom, and children wander among

85

them. When the birds take flight, their wingbeats echo crazily around the marble drum, a song of twenty centuries.

She angles back through the piazza and then zigzags toward Castel Sant'Angelo. Giant stony angels rise on either side of the bridge. The glowing cylinder of the castle floats ahead with its floodlit plague angel Michael astride.

The bridge is also lit by the glow of cell phones held aloft as people photograph the fortress, themselves, and themselves with the fortress, a little stream of glowing blue rectangles channeled between the flowing city-black marble robes of the heavenly host. Below, the river within its ancient banks shines with a light seemingly its own.

Ahead, Agata curves around to Conciliazione, the broad boulevard sloping up to the looming Vatican. Scooters bray past. On the sidewalks, vendors roast chestnuts over glowing oak charcoal braziers. Vendors fry *suppli classico*, steaming little breaded balls of rice filled with ragù and mozzarella. But here she angles left and winds for an hour downstream along streets above the far rim of the river, branching off to Santa Maria in Trastevere and Dante's home-in-exile. She eventually re-crosses the Tiber on the back of the island, penetrates the Jewish Quarter and back into the old city. Dan keeps her in sight, maintaining cautious distance and noise between them.

Just above Via delle Boteghe Oscure, Agata stops before a dance club. It is early – just past ten – but music thumps across the little piazza and the patio jams and roars with wineglass-lifting revelers. She steps inside. A velvet rope cordons a closed dining room edged with a bar and directs traffic to a stone stairwell lit by vibrant, wavy fig and sunflower neon tubes descending.

At the top of the stairs, a man slouches on a wooden stool and a woman stands beside him. They're checking IDs. The line is short. When Dan reaches them, they wave him past, bored. The woman tugs at an eyebrow ring. The man pats pockets for cigarettes or phone.

The walls of the stairway are stone, chiseled by the slaves of Romans, now slathered with posters for DJs and pop bands. Downstairs, under vaulted stone arches lit by starry halogen lights, the room extends off into a vague cloud of sound. The air pulses. Crammed tables fill a series of niches, presumably ancient storage bins, along one wall. Wavering marble flagstones cover the floor, tilting in odd, mild angles underfoot. A large crowd down the center of the room dances in waves.

Dan cannot see Agata in the dark and hue and din. He moves into the crowd since there is only one direction in which to move through the room, turning his shoulders to slide past people shouting and laughing and jumping.

Then he spots her. She is deep in the dancing crowd. She is laughing and jumping and swerving with them. Her expression glows. Her face is raised to the arched stone ceiling, misty above. She disappears in a forest of upraised arms, all swaying in unison like seaweed to the thud and surge. The forest glows red, then violet, then navy. Dan glimpses her once and then again. To him, she seems to radiate. Her hair gleams ruby in the changing light. Dan stands for a minute watching, but realizes he is the only one unmoving in the mass. With them, he begins to bob and sway. No one pays attention to him. No one cares. It is a crowd of college-aged people, a multitude of languages, tourists from all corners of the continent and the Romans who deign to associate with them. He is synchronized with the crowd and the music, but he watches Agata. She faces away, but rotates slowly, coming back around toward him. Absorbed in a vast mass, he sees only occasional glimpses of her hair, her face, her shoulders and arms lifted. He dances with her from afar.

When she emerges from the dance club into the fresh and quiet night, Agata stands in the piazza for a minute regaining her bearings. Then she sets out toward the Capitoline Hill and thence to Piazza Venetia and Corso, thus over the course of the evening making a giant figure-eight lacing the Renaissance and the Middle and Dark Ages and in and out of the Classical period, all in a few kilometers, as is so easy to do in Rome.

Dan trundles behind, keeping his habitual couple of blocks between them, her form melding into later-night crowds and then reappearing, but never difficult for Dan to spot again, accustomed as his eyes have become to her specific shape and movement.

Then, just as she is about to enter her hotel, a man steps from the portal to her. He has apparently been waiting for her. Dan stops a block behind, barely able to see them. Agata and the man converse. Dan advances slowly, approaching behind a line of waiting traffic. She is talking to the silver-haired man. He wears a grey suit. His shoes shine in the headlights of passing cars. As Dan watches, the man hands something to Agata. It appears to be a tube made of some black material. It is about as long as Agata's forearm. She quickly tucks it against her. They part and she enters her hotel. The transaction happens too quickly for Dan to take a photo.

Dan waits on the sidewalk for a half hour, but she does not emerge. Eventually, he circles to a small *tavola calda* where he devours baked rigatoni and spicy fennel sausage. He considers what he has observed, or more precisely what to do with his observation, what to report. He buys a book, *Plays of Luigi*

Pirandello in Italian, the best item he can find at a newsstand, along with a little notebook, a child's flowered blank journal with a little tin latch.

He returns to his room and showers. He types a text: "A. S. in Rome. Met someone on the street who gave her something. No photo." He hesitates a long time before sending this. If his handlers know she met someone and he fails to report it, they may cut him off. He thinks of Gennie. He thinks of the funds in his wallet, his meager stepping-stone back into her world. Either way, he's given them just enough to keep the wheels turning, but not too much. He feels a protective urge. The conversation overheard in Valencia suggested she is under pressure. Perhaps she is in danger. Why he thinks of her in this manner he doesn't know, and he's aware that he thinks this way, and he's aware that he doesn't understand why.

Dan feels like he maneuvers along a tightrope in pitch blackness to an unknown destination.

He has the Bombay and tonic he considered earlier, and then a second. Settled in an armchair with a chilly glass in one hand, he opens the Pirandello. He starts *Six Characters in Search of an Author*, which of course he has read before but long enough ago that it is new to him again. He jots a quote in his new notebook: *Life is full of strange absurdities, which, strangely enough, do not even need to appear plausible, since they are true.*

CHAPTER 15

ROME
8 November, Wednesday

The next morning, Dan finds a text sent the night before which he had not seen because he had fallen asleep: What hotel is she in?

He steps out onto his balcony. Agata is already waiting on the curb for a taxi. He dashes back in, grabs his few belongings, and just as she is pulling away, sprints out of his hotel to flag a taxi of his own, not difficult on Corso in the morning.

At Termini, Agata buys a ticket from a kiosk and goes to platform thirteen where she stands waiting with her silver suitcase upright alongside. The next train leaving from platform thirteen is going to Naples, Dan reads from the display panel. It leaves in forty minutes. As he watches, Agata moves to a nearby bench, opens her suitcase and appears to re-arrange, re-pack. Dan sees the plastic tube as she lays it atop her clothing. It is long enough that it must be placed diagonally to fit.

He withdraws four hundred Euros. He obtains a ticket to Naples from a vending machine and waits around the corner near an Edicola. He buys sparkling water, chocolate, and a copy of *The Economist* from the newsstand. He purchases an Andrea Camilleri detective novel of Sicily and Elena Ferrante's *Those Who Leave and Those Who Stay*. Also, since he has a few more minutes and Agata is staying in one place, seated on the bench and looking at her phone, he steps next door into a small outdoor gear shop and quickly buys a small Fjallraven knapsack and some underwear and socks and a polo shirt. Splurging, he buys a ribby Colmar soft-shell with a hood. He stuffs the clothing, his books, his sunglasses and his journal into the knapsack.

He returns to his watching spot beside the newsstand. A family from India attempts to make purchases and ask questions at the store, the father in tie and tired jacket, mother and grandmother in saris, a colorfully-bundled baby, very young solemn-faced sons and daughters mirroring their parents, alongside a pile of trunk-sized suitcases. No languages intersect.

Dan steps to the counter beside them. He asks them simple questions in his rusty Hindi. They seek diapers, fruit juice, a currency exchange, bathrooms. He converts to Italian and back into Hindi. They are from the north, probably Punjabi, but Dan's familiarity with the four hundred dialects of India is general, not refined. Nevertheless, the transactions conclude successfully, and the father clasps Dan's hand in both of his.

While waiting, Dan sends a text to his handlers: *A.S. train to Naples.* Not long afterward, he receives a reply: *Don't lose track of her!* Oddly, this message with its excited punctuation is written in Spanish, not in the dry French that he had come to expect from Tranchard, previously his presumptive interlocutor.

Back on the platform, Dan sees Agata board. He is the last person to jump onto the train. It departs the city into the rising sun toward Tivoli and then turns south on the more inland of the two principal lines toward Naples. Rome slowly melts, the last of the arcaded aqueducts and random marble mausoleums in copses of beech and rhododendrons sinking into the countryside.

The terrain grows rough and tumble: hummocky rolling farmland, vineyards with hand-stacked stone walls, sharp-colored cows; trucks stopped at crossings with drivers standing by the road pissing and smoking; a big open sky beckoning overhead, the air and land increasingly dry with each kilometer.

Dan's coach is two behind Agata's. The train is all second-class. He is seated on the left side of the car, and thus Monte Cassino, when it hoves into view, rises beside him on the ridge.

Monte Cassino, the monastery destroyed during the war, reminds Dan of tasks left half-completed.

Transient work culling nearby fields had introduced him to the monks, and they soon learned that he spoke many languages. They asked him to help restore part of their library by translating some texts from Romanian. Always in pursuit of work, Dan had left the translation project unfinished, promising to return.

This memory leads to another, and then to another: a chain of well-intentioned undertakings prematurely fractured. He remembers his landlady. He remembers Mariana. He remembers the African men in the park. He remembers many things he has shunted away from, through negligence or exigency.

In this mood, he pulls the little journal and a pen out of his knapsack. He writes *Angelique* at the top of a blank page. Then he starts a list with asterisk bullets, headed, *Why it's for the best:*

- *She blames me for everything. Always will.*
  She's arrogant. Even more than I am.
- *Acts as if I was the first one of us or the only one of us to have an affair. Still acting that way.*
- *Monomaniacal about her body, her training.*
  Acts as if anyone who isn't likewise is flawed.
  Bad breath after working out. So, most of the time.

- *Publicly bragged about my job, my languages, but laughed at me when we were alone. As if we were both just putting on airs.*
- *She never loved me as much as I loved her. Something hollow inside, where all the feeling, passion, politics, family, social justice, beauty should be – everything collapses and disappears.*
- *Her rings are irritating, the way she wears them. Also her necklaces. Her predictable look. The way she ties her shoes. So superior.*
- *I think on balance she always made me unhappy and tense more than she made me happy and comfortable. I can see that now.*
- *She takes maybe two sips of wine and talks about how drunk she is.*
- *Spent a lot of money secretly, but picked through my receipts.*
- *I never liked how she drives. Crowding the center-line. Talking on her phone. She'll kill someone eventually.*
- *She doesn't give people gifts that they want She gives them gifts she thinks they should have.*
- *The sex went away, even before all the bad things happened. Mechanical. Desperate. Brief. Made me feel like a jackass. Little compliments and pats on my shoulders, then nothingness.*
- *She can be funny, but she acts as if I should admire her for that since I'm not funny.*
- *I think she finds me disgusting.*

The list runs onto two of the little pages. He reads through it again and turns his face aside, profoundly dark: unhelpful, shocking, embittering. Nothing new here; just the jotted thoughts of someone churning through the same material for years.

Dan flips a page and starts another list in the journal: *What is the best resolution now?* He makes a bullet point, but does not come up with anything other than to write *GENNIE* in dark letters.

He sits for a while as the train shunts through sidings near Capua. Then he opens another page and makes a third list with no heading. He writes:

- *Dancing.*
- *The way she laughed, and made me laugh.*
- *The night Adrienne was conceived (we think).*
  The way she felt in my hands.
- *Walking in Plaines d'Abraham in the rain not saying anything, night after night. The way we got through everything.*
- *Picking strawberries at that farm with the girls, her straw hat.*
- *In general, a good mother. Tireless.*
- *Watching people watch her.*
- *When she played the piano.*
- *Watching her ride horses. Her eyes. The eyes of the horses.*
- *Sometimes when she saw me.*
- *The smell of her. I miss the smell of her.*

Then he scrawls a heading at the top of the page: *What's wrong with me?*

But, sitting on the train rolling south through Italian rural landscape, sunshine occasionally cracking over scalloped clouds and lifting the hills, Dan turns to a clean page and writes, *A shell is breaking.* He underscores this line twice. He adds, *A fool's errand to be the solitary last soul clinging to a faded and frail old dream.*

The train slows and draws gently into Caserta, with the backside of the vast stark palace rising directly to the left beyond grand dusty yards as they enter the station. In Caserta station, the train is split at the car just ahead of Dan. The rear half where he is sitting, he realizes from the announcement that comes across as the decoupling operation is already underway, is going to Naples. The front half is going to Bari. Dan either read the sign board in Termini incorrectly, or it's just an Italian glitch, the usual. Dan quickly changes cars.

A conductor saw him change trains just as they were pulling out. He comes to Dan's seat and asks to see his ticket. Dan's ticket is for Naples. Dan apologizes.

The conductor explains that typically a fine is involved in such situations. He speaks enough that Dan can identify his accent as northern, Piedmontese, somewhere between Aosta and Varese. Dan asks him about that and then chats for five minutes, about the expense of the lake district, the craziness of Milano, the dullness of Turin, how confusing it is to change trains in Ivrea and how once Dan got on the wrong train there and ended up in France. After the conversation circles through the conductor's concerns about his son's deployment prospects in the army, the conductor sells Dan a discounted ticket to Bari and departs congenially after a handshake between the two.

Views of Vesuvius in the distance break through, framed mistily between plantings of chestnuts and cypresses as in romantic 19th-century paintings. Dan considers sending a text to amend his previous report, namely that Agata was headed to

Naples. Instead, he decides to wait to see where she will alight. He mulls his position. Apparently satisfied with Dan's results so far, his patrons have been paying him. He has amassed enough to buy something substantial for Gennie, or at least a token gift. Perhaps he can make his way to Paris after this task has been completed and render her his daughter again. Something along those lines needs to happen before he can break free, before he can begin anew.

More to the point: He is following a woman who may be involved in the theft of artwork. Every fiber of his moral being cries out for him to expose what he knows. This would restore some order to the world. But to do so would necessitate being interviewed himself. He would be arrested and extradited once they learned who he was. And the little river of money stemming from the reasonably legitimate enterprise of following the woman would end.

Furthermore, and this was not a small consideration for Dan, he could swear either Agata or both of them are being followed by someone else.

Shifting light and the shadows of power poles flicker across his face. This is not a high-speed train like the line from Madrid to Valencia or from Paris to Marseille or from Hanover to Wurzburg. But it moves like silk and the landscape melts behind as Dan watches idly, no longer interested in making notes or even reading. A light haze of smoke from chimneys and slash piles hangs in layers over the flattening ground. The smell of it even reaches vaguely into the train car. Before long, light rain begins, streaking the windows in long horizontal lines.

It's late afternoon when the Frecciabianca train gently curves past Barletta and straightens southerly along the coast. Occasional glimpses of the sea afford a meager ocean view, shards of breakers in landwash glow and further out a green starboard light or two signal boat traffic, moving under a moon peeking bright-eyed from a black cloud burka. Along the shore, the rain has relented.

It's gloaming when, south of Bisceglie, the line runs past an amusement park, ablaze, sparkling, tumultuous in the cloaked night landward. A carousel coruscates. A coaster arches and drops parallel. For a moment, the speed of the ride matches that of the train, and for a viewer like Dan in the delirium of night, it's as if the conveyances exchange places.

CHAPTER 16

BARI
8 November, Wednesday

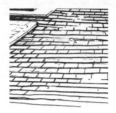

In Bari Centrale, the train disgorges its meager agglomeration of passengers under the platform floodlights, including Agata, and subsequently, Dan. She has exchanged the black coat for the yellow again and has donned a scarf with a vivid red paisley pattern. She walks to the taxi line and climbs into a car. Dan closes the distance between them at a run and takes a taxi in the row behind as hers circles away and onto Niccolo del Arca. They skirt the grand park fronting the university, dotted with strollers at this time of the evening celebrating midweek, but then peel off toward the old city.

The two taxis are from the same company. Dan's driver holds his phone in his hand as he steers through traffic, scrolling numbers. He is suspicious of Dan's request to follow but not too closely. Perhaps he is considering calling the other cab or the dispatcher. Eventually he states baldly, "If you're stalking someone, I don't want any part of it." His accent is Neapolitan.

Dan quickly invents a story. "We don't want her husband to see us," he says. This makes sense to the driver and he visibly relaxes.

The taxi's windows are open. The damp, post-storm air carries fragrances sharply: ocean, grilling beef, baking bread, fish, lemon, old wet stone. Agata's driver deposits her with her suitcase at the ferry terminal. She enters the Jadrolinija building.

In the ticket office, she sits at an agent's desk and talks for what seems a long time. The agent shows her schedules, a brochure, which she ignores. Dan can tell by the angle of her shoulders that she is impatient. He sees her take things from her purse, buy a ticket. He waits until she finishes. Near him, before the terminal, a group of musicians – mandolin, guitar, accordion, tambourines – plays frenetically before a small crowd. The music is pure tarantella, and joyous. Rhythm and tempo throb; a few dancers bounce. Children slalom among legs. A circle of old men bobs, their eyes closed as in rapture, or remembrance.

After she has left the office, Dan quickly enters and buys a ticket to Dubrovnik. The agent dawdles. Dan keeps looking over his shoulder after her as Agata waits at the corner and then crosses into the night towing her suitcase. Purchase completed, he runs after her. He spots her in a café up the street just inside the city wall seated at a table near the window having a coffee. He watches from across the street in the shadows of a jewelry store awning, lounging against an old wall. They have two hours to expend.

A man passes the café in which Agata sits. He pauses, seems to spot her and then keeps moving. He stops a few paces beyond, turns back and watches the café in which Agata sits. He smokes. Dan recognizes, or possibly recognizes, his figure. No details, just the shape of him. From across the street, Dan takes out his phone, zooms, clicks a quick photo just before the man moves away. It is a clear profile, the dark eye sockets, the mustache, the cigarette.

Back at the ferry terminal, he waits in line far behind Agata. At least fifty people separate them, a few tourists British and

French, mostly; a few Italians; a few Croats and Serbs; mountains of suitcases.

After Dan joins the line, a young Chinese couple towing matching suitcases races up behind him. They are agitated. They talk fast and high to each other, ranging around for signs they can understand, information of any kind. Dan has only a small vocabulary in Standard Chinese, collected like curios, and little grammar. The mutually unintelligible variations confound him, Cantonese, Huanese, Min, Wu. But he gathers the couple is unsure if they are in the right place, if their tickets are correct, if their documents are in order – logical concerns.

Dan asks if he can be of assistance and in broken Mandarin helps them through logistical questions. The man and woman are desperately grateful. They offer him money. The woman eventually gives him a bookmark embroidered with a dragon and stork and the *hanzi* for love and luck.

He remembers an older colleague at CSIS, also a language specialist and Dan's mentor, who once recited for Dan a quote from Salman Rushdie: *Translation means bearing across. Having been borne across the world, we are translated men. It is normally supposed that something always gets lost in translation; I cling, obstinately to the notion that something can also be gained.*

Eventually, blue-suited women with nametags allow the line of passengers to ascend long ramps to more waiting areas, queue for passport control, check through ticket scanners and advance into elevated gangway tunnels leading to the ship. Agata disappears to an upper deck, signifying that she has a private cabin for the night. Dan will sleep in a chair.

The ferry slips from the quay, bow thrusters boiling. Thick, looped hawsers splash into the harbor and are drawn into the ship by fast windlasses fore and aft. Dan stands out on the starboard deck to watch the dock crew. Departing the harbor, the vessel rounds the breakwater and points northeast into an overcast night.

Dan stays on the forward deck alone a long time in the wind. The ship's bow wake plunges and crashes fifteen meters below. Mostly, Dan watches the lights of a handful of small boats, fishing trawlers and skiffs, probably, since pleasure traffic season has long dwindled for the year, although a large ketch, with genoa and main bellied in the southerly wind and glowing in its masthead light, heads north along the coast, possibly to Ancona or even Venice. The ferry swings slightly to cross behind it.

Dan remembers to send a message before passing out of cell range: *A.S. leaving Bari by ferry for Dubrovnik.* After a minute, a reply appears: *Why didn't you tell us where you were?* Dan does not reply to this message for a while, and soon his phone shows no cell reception.

The lights of Italy soon vanish in the brawly sea haze behind them and he is alone on the windswept deck in the black of the Adriatic. He turns to look upward through heavy reverse-sloped windshields at the enclosed bridge, where the face of the officer of the watch, guessing from her epaulets, glows green in the radar light. She turns and speaks to a seaman nearby, presumably her lookout, a small joke between sea-mates. They laugh.

Cumulatively, Dan spent years of his life aboard boats, sailing on rivers, lakes and reservoirs, on bays, estuaries and sounds, on open seas and oceans.

He skippered everything from dinghies barely longer than he is tall to yachts fifty meters in length with staterooms the size of small apartments. He crewed sailing vessels and power vessels, private and commercial.

Embedded in that world, one invitation turns into another, since boats, expensive objects of desire and myth, are always going somewhere and crew is evanescent, always in short supply. Dan's racing background provided cachet. Boat owners viewed his Olympic medals, a silver and a bronze, like law firms view Harvard diplomas. One yacht owner would introduce Dan to another, saying, "He can handle your boat; he won medals in Barcelona." Notwithstanding the fact that his racing background was mostly on little one-designs, Stars and Lasers and Sunfish, even Hobies, he was constantly placed at the helm of big yachts, which he also sailed smoothly and fast.

He was a congenial skipper. Crews responded well to him. Boats he commanded usually rounded their marks in the lead or arrived at their destinations safely and quickly and on budget.

Notwithstanding, he also displayed a reckless streak that emerged in competitive moments. His eyes blazed when challenged by wind, wave, or racer with that peculiar inner light that radiates from powerful competitors. Under pressure, excited, he took risks that other yachtsmen would not, cutting angles, slamming on sail, over-powering into steep seas and close shaves, driving machinery and crew beyond physical limits. He won races this way.

In some cases, predictably, the trait brought catastrophe, ranging from broken rigs in small offshore regattas and in the Fastnet to dumping a boat onto a reef off Wellington and a notable collision in Port Phillip near Melbourne which injured three crew and made the evening news.

And running the family's little sailboat into a too-strong wind with broken rudder mounts, his fourteen-year-old daughter Adrienne at the helm alone because he was excited and filled with the thrill of a blustery day. She joined his exuberance because she felt his adoration for her being there with him, for being who she was. She trusted that the boat would withstand its next test because her dad said it would. Momentary misjudgment; a price exacted forever.

102

Land-bound in Madrid the previous year, the swell of the sea beneath his feet again reinvigorates a long slate of memories this evening. But there is nothing to be gained from such reminiscing, especially since each trail of successes seems to spiral ultimately onto a red-hot failure. Wind-lashed and beaten, after a while he slips back inside and settles into a seat in one of the rows in the mostly empty forward saloon of the ferry.

CHAPTER 17

AT SEA
8 November, Wednesday

Dan dozes until almost midnight. When he wakes, he descends to the cafeteria. At the register, Agata is paying for a salad and an Aqua Panna. Carrying these, she leaves the tray, skirts the dining room and winds back to the stairwell heading to the upper decks of cabins.

Dan takes a tray and selects macaroni and a salad. The food is dejected, half-warm, as is the sole employee in the cafeteria. He sits in the dining room. He is alone among a hundred empty tables. The seas have picked up and the deck rises and slumps noticeably. Out in the seating areas, passengers like him who did not take cabins turn uncomfortably under blankets and coats, watch droning televisions: Croatian-dubbed Italian movies, Zagreb football. A baby cries. Vague scents of vomit and bleach crawl through the overheated air.

The slow roll of the deck underfoot pulls Dan backward.

After his family's disintegration, clawing out of blinding depression, Dan took a serendipitous job offer as second in command on a late-season delivery of a racing sloop, a custom-built, thirty-meter-long, fifty-meter-masted monster, from the Chesapeake to the Mediterranean. They came into the harbor of Marseille after eleven days at sea, the crew of five in rebounding spirits after a dreary ocean slog. At sea, numerous clouds seemed to have lifted from Dan. They stepped onto the customs dock, in the broad channel behind Quai Jean Charcot outside the old harbor, and chatted with the officer who filled out forms, inspected their passports, inquired after plant products, endangered animal and plant species, cultural goods, arms and ammunition.

Dan, the only French-speaker among the crew, carried the conversation with the customs staff: No quarantine required since the boat had come directly from the United States; fees to be paid; the speed and comfort of the crossing; seas, winds, weather, traffic; latest doings in Marseille, especially the win-loss record of Olympique in Ligue 1.

Dan had taken a two-month leave from CSIS. Angelique had left for Paris earlier that year with Genevieve, then not yet thirteen. Dan aimed to go to Paris to visit them, possibly to talk things over a little more with Angelique, to sound out whether the time passing had opened any windows. He planned to fly, but then the crew job appeared. If he had flown, his life would have been very different now.

The customs officer took down individual passport information and ticked the boxes on the forms indicating that all identification papers were in order. But perhaps this information never made it into larger systems, or at least not immediately. If it had, Dan would have been pulled aside.

While on the Atlantic crossing, a warrant had been issued in Canada for his arrest. The falsehoods that he, an officer of the law, told on the stand during the trial of a murderer in Vancouver had been revealed within a quiet investigation. A man had gone to prison based on Dan's false testimony.

Dan did not learn of the warrant until he spoke with Angelique in Paris. French police had contacted Angelique, as had people from the Canadian Embassy. But at the time they reached her, she did not know where Dan was.

It was not until two weeks later that he showed up one evening at her apartment on Rue Garanciere just above Jardin du Luxembourg. They sat at her kitchen table. She said, "You committed perjury? You're many things, Dan, but you're not a liar. What's become of you?"

He cried. He wiped his face.

She said, "Just go. If they ask again, I'll tell them I haven't seen you."

That was seven years before this night on the Jadrolinija ferry, give or take a few weeks. November, anyway. The trees along Saint Germain hung bare. Lights in cafés went on shortly after lunch. He left Paris on foot, hitchhiking with his sea duffel between truck stops in the rain on the A-4 toward Reims. He continued to Germany. He did not know why, or what he would do there. Some vague notion appealed to him of little stone-clad towns with winding streets, smoky fireplaces, deep evergreen embraces, the smells of beer and wool. These bone-memory sensations fed his need to survive.

By the time the ship has reached the middle of the Adriatic, two in the morning, the seas have diminished. The decks rumble quietly. Passengers snore in their seats under their jackets. Dan finally drifts into hazy sleep.

CHAPTER 18

DUBROVNIK
9 November, Thursday

Ferries come deep into Dubrovnik harbor and dock closer to the city than the cruise ships, closer even than the towering mega-yachts tied sterns to the quay with their uniformed crews polishing topsides. Still it is a long walk over the saddle between the ridge and peninsula of the newer town to the upper gate of the old city. In view of this, Agata takes a taxi outside the three-meter chain-link and barbed wire fence for the three-minute ride.

Indeed, when Dan arrives, she is still on the bridge over the city's moat as if waiting, photographing the limestone walls, the chasm and the ocean beyond with her phone. Hordes of tourists stream down into the city, but nothing like during the height of the summer.

Agata puts away her phone and tows her silver suitcase down the snaking walkway between outer and inner walls into the city past charts showing where Serb mortar shells, lobbed from the high ridge above, hit during the Yugoslav wars.

Agata ascends the steps of a narrow street, Siroka, to the south under window boxes barren of flowers for the winter. The morning sun lies across her face, and she shades her eyes. She finds an address and rings the bell. A woman comes to the door and lets her in. Once the door has closed, Dan slips past on the narrow stairstep street and reads the sign by the doorbell: a guesthouse.

Dan's next move is again uncertain. While Agata gets situated, he returns to Stradun, withdraws twenty-nine hundred and eighty kuna, the equivalent of four hundred Euros, at a bank machine, then, at a café, gets a coffee and a couple of *palatschinke* covered in powdered sugar. He speaks with the doe-eyed woman at the counter at length, mostly to practice Croatian, which he handles with decreasing difficulty as he sifts through old mental file cabinets, beginning to restore vocabulary, turns of phrase. He returns to the narrow street. There is a small square in front of a church, with a fountain and tree. He sits on a bench under the tree. Agata will probably return via this route.

He texts his handlers the name and address of the guesthouse in which Agata is staying. Then he waits on the bench.

Agata does come by this way, eventually. But not before Dan finishes Ferrante and gets halfway through Camilleri, eats half of the chocolate bar he purchased in Rome, thinks about getting more food but instead falls asleep under his coat. The whole day is gone, he discovers, awakened by the sound of her shoes. She clips past down the limestone steps in her green jeans, her black coat, the maroon scarf which reflects her hair color. He rolls and sees the back of her black coat as she turns the corner.

No rain yet, but the sky is now sealed. The sun has nearly set, the mid-Med almost as cold as it gets. In the streets of Dubrovnik, the bulk of tourists have left and a few locals and overnighters stroll. Store lights remain on; a few window signs announce upcoming Christmas discounts. Families push strollers and greet each other. A lone truck, a tiny one-seater loaded with beer kegs, mumbles up Stradun. It provides the only mechanical noise in this city, apart from the bells at Saint Blaise.

Agata heads in that direction, downhill, along the inverted spine between the clasped ribs of the town. She turns left and begins the climb on the other side, angles through the narrowing streets to flights of stone steps, then along the street which traces the interior base of the city wall. Darkness has thoroughly settled, and the footing in spaces between street lamps on stone walls is felt rather than seen.

She comes to a doorway in the wall. It is the entrance to a bar which hangs from the cliff on the outside of the wall, planted on a series of terraced rocks above the ocean. It is a place popular with tourists during the day and with romantic locals at night after the day-trippers have departed. There is no sign, just a rusted steel doorway propped open.

Stepping through the doorway in the ancient wall, a grated landing overlooks the bar's tables and roof below and the tossing grey sea foaming the rocks lower still. Steps descend first angling right, then left.

DUBROVNIK
9 November, Thursday

Dan stands on the little landing at the top. Agata has descended to the covered bar area and has already taken a seat overlooking the bay.

The sea scintillates in stormy early moonlight. A few lights toss from yachts anchored in the gap between Lokrum and the mainland. The terraces lie dark but for some candles and the stars of cigarettes. Low voices rise from below, calm chatting over the slow break of waves on the rocks.

He descends the steps to the corner. He remembers this place from years before as a small enterprise with a few tables scattered down the cliffside behind steel railings, exposed and intimate at the same time. A person at one of the tables, with a glance over a shoulder, has a full view of everyone descending the cliffside to the bar.

He takes the risk because it is dark. He seats himself at the end nearest the landing and sets his knapsack on the ground. A waitress brings him wine.

He looks over at Agata. She sits alone at the far end, her face candlelit, staring out at the evening sea. She sips a drink in a cut-glass tumbler. He sees her draw a deep breath, the rise of her chest. As he looks at her, she slowly turns and looks at him. They look at each other down the long bar for an extended, unbroken moment.

Little votive candles in glass jars flicker in brushstrokes of breeze. They compose the only true light, clusters on tables like tiny warm galaxies. He turns back to the sea and for several minutes watches the endless pewter nothingness of the Mediterranean beyond the island.

Then he hears the scrape of a nearby chair. He turns, and there is Agata sitting directly beside him. She turns her chair so her knees almost touch his. Her features are vague in the gloom, but her eyes sparkle candlelight. She looks at him for a moment, and then laughs shortly at the expression on his face. But she turns out to face into the darkness, and her voice when she speaks is not mirthful.

"We're in trouble," she says. "We need to stop."

"I know," he says.

PART TWO

CHAPTER 20

DUBROVNIK
9 November, Thursday

Daniel David Durand and Agata Alma Svendson sit side-by-side on low bar chairs behind a dark railing for a full minute. They both watch the slow, off-silver sea. Candleflames clustered in the little glass jars lean and writhe. The faces of the people cup with shadows in this shifting light.

Dan's expressions proceed through a series of processes. Agata glances at him. His eyes invoke the gauze-wrapped moon which reflects off the ocean. Eventually he starts to speak, clears his throat and then says, "Why?"

She intuits the subject of the question. "Trail of bread crumbs," she says lowly and evenly. "A diversion."

More silence ensues. Then she adds, "But I don't trust them. Never did. Things have changed, and now they're falling apart. I can't take this anymore. I'm scared. I can't continue doing what I was supposed to be doing, and I don't know what to do next."

"What were you supposed to be doing?"

"Leading you. Taking you on a slow trip with a few waypoints. You use the debit card along the way, use the passport. Leave digital trails that trackers can get to. From here we were supposed to go up into Mostar, Sarajevo, then across to

115

Belgrade, Timisoara and Bucharest. Then Chisinau. The police follow you. That was the plan. That was my assignment. You're my assignment, and I'm yours."

"Why me?"

"You look just like him."

"Who?"

"Alvaro Rodriguez."

The slight wind has lifted. Once and again, stronger waves punch the rocks a dozen meters below their feet and then settle in soft shuffles. Scud crosses the moon.

Dan says, "I was told you were going somewhere to meet people who had stolen a painting. A Magritte. They said you were involved in the theft."

"Magritte?" She sniffs. "Very creative of Tranchard. I figured they'd feed you some story like that, but they didn't fill me in. They just told me where to go. What they gave you was a decoy story. No painting was taken from them. Or rather, at the time they were talking to you, no painting had been taken. But one has been taken now. I have it."

Dan sits quietly. He allows her space to expand on this.

"It's in my room. In my suitcase." She sips her drink. "My friend Henri took it from Alvaro day before yesterday, in the morning. He gave it to me that evening. In Rome. He passed it to me for safekeeping. I'm supposed to hang onto it temporarily and keep moving. He said he would meet me, but I haven't heard from him since I last saw him. I called him, texted him. Nothing." She tilts her glass and finishes her drink and then swivels to look for the waiter. Since the bar is mostly empty, he comes to her immediately. She orders another gin and lime. While waiting for it, she wraps her coat tighter.

He has not seen her this close. Her face is softer than in the photo he was shown, the angles less severe. Her reddish hair falls in curved bangs to her eyebrows. She wears no makeup, or if she does it's very light. There is a lift to her chin, her head angled slightly back as she looks at him.

"Tell me about the painting you have," Dan says.

"It's called *Pastoral*. It's a Matisse. It's about a hundred years old. It was in a museum in Paris. The Musée d'Artes Moderne. It was stolen from the museum a few years ago. That one, along with some others. They were never recovered. The thieves were caught later. They said the paintings had been destroyed long before. But they lied."

"Thieves have been known to do that."

"The paintings weren't lost. Alvaro Rodriguez ended up with the Matisse. He showed it to me once. I work for him, you know. I do odd jobs for him, mostly research. I'm a researcher."

Dan eats an olive. Church bells ring softly.

He says, "I remember reading about the robbery in Paris. It happened just before I moved to Europe, so probably 2010. So there was no Magritte?"

Agata shakes her head. "They were lying to you," she says. Her voice has settled into liquid. She looks down at the tabletop and then up at Dan. "Alvaro had the Matisse. I don't know how he got it. Henri said he killed people for it. Alvaro was trying to slip away somewhere with it. I don't know where. I know he has connections in South America, family and so forth. He had Tranchard and Franco hire you to follow me to throw the police off his track. Alvaro wanted someone, a dupe, really – sorry about that – to travel across the continent toward the east using Alvaro's ID, his passport and his credit card, or debit card.

In particular, they wanted a person who could be physically mistaken for Alvaro."

She tips her glass and drains it. "Your photo is taken when you use bank machines, when you go through security lines. You have to show a passport to get a hotel room. So there's an electronic trail of your movements and your face which could be tracked by someone who could get into those systems. What Alvaro needed was someone they could hire to do this job, to travel across the continent leaving markers. Or someone they could trick into doing it. The idea was that the police would chase the decoy, meaning you, while Alvaro vanishes from Madrid with the Matisse. You were the perfect choice."

She swirls the ice in its glass. She says, "The police were getting close to Alvaro. I heard Tranchard talking to him about it. I warned Henri because I didn't want him to get hurt."

Agata pauses as the other customers pass behind them before resuming in a voice just above a whisper.

"It was purely an accident that they ran across you. Specifically, one of the girls in that café you go to a lot in Madrid is a former roommate of a daughter of one of these people. She knew Alvaro from parties or whatever. She commented to someone one day that a guy was coming into the café who looked just like Alvaro. The first couple of times, she thought it was him. But it was you."

Dan remembers the tall girl in the café greeting him by a different name one morning shortly after he went there the first time and met Mariana. He had corrected her and she cheerfully apologized as she made his perfect cortado.

Agata smiles at Dan and says, "You look enough like him that when I came out of the bathroom in the Valencia airport and saw you standing there it freaked me out. For a moment

I thought you were Alvaro. Scared the hell out of me. Then I realized it was you and I was so relieved. A friendly face.

"You're a little taller but about the same," Agata continues, "same general build, same basic structure. At the time you also had a grey beard, like he does. So anyway, they started looking into you. They asked questions, starting in the café. They found out you were sort of itinerant, but also had a deep background. They became very interested in you. They had me research you. It took a couple of weeks. I felt like I came to know you. You're not a low-life, like them. I was worried for you when I told them what I found out about you, your background. That's why I'm telling all of this to you now. I'm down to the bitter end on people I can trust. There's you, because I don't think you are going to hurt me, and there's Henri. And I don't know where he is."

"Who is Henri?"

"He's a former doctor. A thoracic surgeon. He was once prominent. He was even in Médecins Sans Frontières for a while. He's a good man. But he fell on difficulties. He's never told me all the details. Alvaro got his hooks into him somehow. Alvaro finds ways to do that. So Henri has been working for Alvaro over the past year or two, sort of like I have. Doing odd jobs. Afraid of saying no."

Dan says, "Why did Henri take this Matisse from Alvaro?"

"He said it needed to be done. It needs to be returned. Like I said, he's a good man. He's also very French. The Matisse is a part of France."

"If he knew Alvaro had the painting, why didn't he just call the police?"

"He said he thought that Alvaro was planning to run with it before the police could get there. Alvaro was on the verge. Henri was in the apartment; Alvaro stepped out but would be back momentarily. Henri only had a few minutes to decide. That's what he told me. He ran to the airport, caught an evening flight to Rome and handed the painting to me."

"Why did he give it to you instead of to the police?" Dan has leaned forward and rested his chin in his hand. Their faces are close and they speak in whispers, but his expression belies doubt.

"He didn't have time to explain that to me standing on the street in Rome. He just said to keep quiet, move along, don't say anything to anyone. He said not to turn it in to the police yet. He would do that with me to make sure it went smoothly. If I did it without him there, the police might not believe me. He had to get back to Madrid to clean up. That's how he put it."

"So Henri met you in Rome to give you the painting. Why did he meet you earlier in Cuenca and again in Èze?"

"In Cuenca, I called him because I wanted to talk to him. I wanted to warn him in person that I thought something weird was happening. I was doing this job because I was afraid of saying no to them. They are frightening people, you know. But I was also growing afraid that by doing the job I was digging my own grave. Then Henri called me the next day and said to meet him in Èze. He drove all night to get over there. I think he just wanted to reassure me, tell me to hang in there, keep going. We only talked for a minute or two there. Then the next afternoon he called me and said he'd meet me that night at my hotel."

"Why did Henri meet you all three times in person right out in the open, including when he gave you the painting, when you both knew I'd be watching and would report it to Tranchard?"

"That was Henri's idea. He said it would be safer for all of us if it appeared we weren't hiding." She pauses for a minute. A fragment of laughter rises from some couples down the bar, and the clink of glassware. Apart from that, only church bells and soft surf rub against the night.

"You don't think I'm telling you the truth," Agata says.

"I don't think anyone has been telling me the truth."

Dan looks around the terraces of the bar. He looks up the stairs over his shoulder. Just then a figure emerges onto the landing from the doorway of the stone passage through the city wall. As Dan's did when he came through, the person's eyes must adjust from the relative brightness under the streetlamp to the dark of the cliffside bar lit only by handfuls of candles and the remainder of the moon. For a minute, the figure is blinded by nothingness.

"Go," Dan says to Agata. She looks around. "Go now," he insists. "I'll catch up later." She stands and takes her purse and climbs the steps quickly. The figure is still standing on the landing when she passes him. The man steps aside for her, then turns to look after her as she enters the passage. He looks around at the flickery darkness below, then follows Agata back into the street.

Dan climbs the steps, passes through the tunnel in the wall and peeks around the corner. The street lies vacant and silent both directions. He waits by the iron door in the shadows for a couple minutes with only the sound of the soft music and voices from behind him accompanied by gentle surf on the rocks. His next move is unclear, since he doesn't want to follow her immediately back to her hotel, so he turns right and descends slowly to Stradun and walks its length, and then back. This absorbs a total of fifteen minutes. The evening crowds have thinned. Most shops have closed. Bells sound once more from Saint Blaise and from Katedrala Uznesenja Marijina, tucking in the town.

121

CHAPTER 21

DUBROVNIK
9 November, Thursday

Dan walks back uphill toward the guesthouse where Agata is staying. He looks right and left and behind, constantly. At each intersecting pedestrian alley, he peers around the corner before advancing. A few stray walkers pass, a few cats. In the narrow street before her guesthouse, he passes without stopping, walking slowly. No lights are on in the front room, which through the glass door appears to be a living area backed by a kitchen counter, but light pours from the next window. It's a bedroom. On a luggage rack lies the silver suitcase, opened. He stops, looks all around, up and down the narrow stairstep street. Then he taps lightly on the window. Another tap is required before Agata appears from an adjacent room. She undoes the latches and swings open the window a hand's breadth. "Bring your things," he says. "We have to get out of here."

Wearing the black coat and carrying her suitcase up the stepped street, she meets him at the top a few minutes later. She glances all around, breathing quickly.

"You're sure no one is watching us?"

"No. But let's take our chances," he says.

They descend on a veering pattern through little streets and squares and then ascend through the city gate. Agata is flushed from the climb and stops to remove her scarf and tuck it in a pocket. They walk together along the road uphill toward a large turnaround where a pair of taxis loiter. They climb into one and are driven up and over the crest of the ridge.

Dan asks the driver to turn onto Vojnovica, which threads out onto the peninsula, and to drive very slowly. He watches behind them, but their car is alone on the road. He instructs the taxi to loop down toward the park and then pull over and stop. They sit in silence for several minutes, the driver drifting around on his phone, the fare blinking slowly upward. Only one car passes; three teenagers coming up from the park, laughing.

"I don't see anyone. I think we lost him," Dan says.

"Hopefully he's as bad at following people as you are," Agata says.

Dan considers the layers of this observation. "I've never excelled at following," he says at last. "Fortunately, you're a gentle leader."

Presently, Dan asks the driver to take them to one of the hotels on the hill overlooking the sea. It is a sprawling resort property, brightly lit all around, staff on duty all night, doormen and security guards, a sapphire swimming pool under the stars, vacant, stacks of thick towels folded on chairs. At reception, Dan asks for two rooms. But they are both too electrified to sleep. So, he carrying his knapsack and she towing her suitcase, they enter the mostly vacant lounge and seat themselves at the bar. Russian businessmen crowded around a table near a fireless fireplace laugh loudly at jokes among themselves. A woman delivers drinks on a wicker tray. When her martini is placed before her, Agata finishes half of it immediately.

Dan says, "I want to see it."

She looks down at her suitcase and then up at him. "Kind of amazing, isn't it?" she says. "Hard to believe. It's right there beside us. A priceless work of art, and such a colorful history." She looks around the room.

"Not now. Not here," Dan says. He sips his drink. "Let's just talk for a while. I think between us you hold most of the cards. Is Agata Svendson your real name?"

She nods. "Agata Alma Svendson. Danish name, but I'm from New York."

"Who is Alvaro Rodriguez?"

"A middle-weight criminal. At least I think he's a criminal. He never gave me any reason to doubt it. The name may be an alias. He's not Spanish, but he's been in Madrid a long time. I've talked to him on the phone. I've never met him. But I've seen pictures."

"You said he looks like me? Or I look like him."

She nods. "But with a beard. Grey beard. Very handsome guy. Like a vampire. He sounds like Dracula, too. And I honestly think he's killed people, like I said before." She drinks the balance of her martini.

"There's one thing you need to know," she inserts into the ensuing silence, "just so you understand the sort of people we're dealing with. If you hadn't accepted the assignment willingly for what they're paying you, and that amount is pocket change to them, they probably would have made you do it. I mean grabbed you one night and made you. They knew that you're drifting, undocumented, unconnected, wanted in Canada. They figured they could use you one way or another. But that would have been a lot more difficult and potentially messier than just tricking you into working for them. I have this on good authority."

"Who is Tranchard?"

"Alvaro's lawyer. I looked him up one time. He was disbarred in Belgium and the Netherlands. Shyster, but very smart."

"Who is Franco?"

"An enforcer. Idiot. He once almost broke my arm. I was arguing with them and he took my arm in his hand and just squeezed. I couldn't use my hand for a couple days. I think I still have the bruise. He just grinned at me. But of the two of them, Tranchard scares me more."

Dan signals to the bartender. In Croatian, he asks her for more drinks and some bread and oil.

"How many languages do you speak?" Agata says.

He lifts his hands and shrugs. "Fluently? Fourteen, fifteen, depending on the layers of rust. A couple dozen more just at a book level, meaning I know vocabulary and grammar, I can understand things but couldn't carry a conversation."

"So many languages out there."

Dan arches his eyebrows. "Four-hundred and forty-five living Indo-European languages, and that's just six percent of the world's total."

"Besides English, I only speak some schoolgirl French and Spanish. How did you start learning them?"

"My parents were Czech expatriates. They fled to Canada after the collapse in 1968. At one point, they changed their last name from Železný, an old Czech name signifying strength, to Durand, a French equivalent. I grew up in a small town in southern Quebec amid English, French and Czech. I was the sort of child who speaks in full, lucid sentences, startling all the adults. I understand that some brains are preternaturally polyglot. By age five I could maneuver easily among those languages. By the age of nine I started adding more. Kids create gothic hiding places, spaces of safety. I had fortress walls of language."

The bartender brings bread on a wooden trencher. They bite into pieces. As two more martinis are placed on napkins before them, Agata asks, "Are you beginning to trust me?"

Dan settles back on his stool. He folds his arms and studies the rows of colorful bottles along the backbar. "I have no reason to trust anyone. You could be telling me the truth. Tranchard could be telling me the truth. If you're in cahoots with them, that would change the complexion of this conversation immensely. I was set up once. Perhaps this is all a further setup, part of a plan, either the one you described, or a larger one, or a completely different one. Maybe you've been paid off by someone else, some unnamed third party. You could even be with the police, which would be fine, though I doubt the police have become this aimless."

He pauses and takes a bite of bread, a sip of his drink. Then he continues.

"I have nothing to go on. All I see is a veil of deceits, and there are only two little pinprick eyeholes of logical truth through that veil: One, someone is lying to me, either Tranchard or you, and two, somebody has certainly been paying me. I have a lot of cash in my wallet that wasn't there a few days ago. Everything else is a cloud of unknowing, as the medieval poet would say. You see my dilemma."

Dan observes her as she struggles with these comments for several minutes. Her face changes shading a few times in the amber bar light. She twists her glass stem and her eyes lift from her hand to his face and back. Eventually she raises her palms in a supplicating shrug, her face open, acquiescent, dismayed.

"I have no way to prove that I'm telling you the truth," she says. "If you want to go, just go. I'll tell them you just vanished."

He says presently, "But to that point, what's your connection to them? And why are you talking to me now?"

She sets down her cocktail and begins. "Alvaro owns me. Some relative of his in America tipped him off that I was in Copenhagen where I was trying to hide. His lawyer, Tranchard, found me there. I was living there with an aunt, trying to stay basically undercover. But he showed up one day, waiting for me in a café around the corner from the library on Slotsholmgade where I liked to sit and read each morning."

She lifts her glass by the stem and takes a long sip, elevates the glass to the backbar light and sights through its steamy torso. "That's a good martini," she says. "It's rare to get good ones in Europe except in American bars in fancy hotels. Usually half vermouth."

She sets the glass on its napkin and places her palms on her face for a moment and then sweeps back her hair the way he saw her do it in the restaurant the first night he followed her.

She continues. "Tranchard offered me a job. I suppose it was something along the lines of when he offered you a job. He didn't ask me about my circumstances, and I didn't offer. But he dropped hints that suggested he knew more than he was saying, chilly little comments. The job he offered was to dig into records of a public official in Belgium. He had some cover story about opposition research, a political thing. He offered good money, and at the time I had nothing. I was living off my aunt. I didn't even own a bicycle."

A man passes behind them. Agata looks down to the suitcase on the floor beside her.

"But then they had another job for me, and another," she continues once the man has passed. "The tasks seemed slimier and slimier. Research on drug lords, corruption. At one point they wanted me to write a dossier on a corporate president, specifically on his family and the daily activities of his wife and little kids. I said no. That was the first time I talked to Alvaro. He called me. He told me they knew about my past. With that Dracula voice, he said straight out that if I didn't want certain people to know where I was living, I would do the work for them.

"They had me move from Copenhagen to Madrid so they could watch me, or specifically have Franco watch me. He would turn up at random times every other day, standing in the street outside the apartment for a few hours, just watching me. I saw him kill a pigeon."

Loud laughter erupts from the group of men near the fireplace. Both Dan and Agata turn and glance at them, but they are clearly laughing among themselves. One mugs and speaks in falsetto for his companions, something about flight attendants.

"I was in my apartment," Agata says, now almost whispering, "and he was standing by the wall across the street. The pigeon came walking by and he suddenly stomped on it. It was horrible. No reason at all. Some people saw him do it and started shouting, but he just turned and walked away with that smirk on his face. Did you see that look when they talked to you?"

"I think I did," Dan says.

"He was measuring you up. I wondered if the pigeon thing was for my benefit since the second after he did it, he sort of looked up at my window. Around then they had me doing other little things, delivering items to people, carrying messages. It was always a carrot-stick scenario. They were paying me sporadically, even giving me little bonuses. This watch, for instance, which is likely stolen. They let me live in the apartment and paid all the bills. But there was always the threat of exposure hanging over me, and if I bristled at anything, they would reinvigorate it."

Dan listens to Agata carefully. He leans forward, one arm on the bar, his hand cupped over his mouth, studying. Agata pauses, looking at him looking at her.

"Then a few weeks back," she says "Alvaro called me, probably the third or fourth time I'd spoken to him, and asked me to go to the Caribbean with him. An indefinite trip. He said he had a yacht in St. Vincent and we would stay on it for a while and then maybe go down to Caracas. He made it clear that in addition to being his personal secretary, his plan was that this would be an intimate arrangement."

She shifts on her barstool, re-hooks her heels on the foot-ring and clamps her thighs tightly together.

"He'd never even met me, but he said I was his type, that we'd get along. He said he could tell these things without meeting people but just by looking at their photos. It was horrible. I told him I was unable to have sex, a physical problem, a hysterectomy gone bad, headaches, sickness, terrible spells, bleeding and infection that I needed drugs for, that I'd had bouts with breast cancer and was all scarred up, in pain, on medication. I was making it up as I went.

"I was desperate not to go. The next week they came to me and told me about this assignment, the assignment with you. The way they talked to me, Tranchard and Franco, it seemed like something final. They didn't speak about anything happening after this job, as they usually do. Once I got you to Chisinau there was no talk of coming back from Moldova. I asked specifically about that, but they said nothing."

The bartender moves past, wiping the counter. He glances at Agata and she nods. She continues in a low, level voice, catching for the first time her own image in the backbar mirror.

"Plus, the timing. This came up shortly after I rejected Alvaro. That's why I think my time is up. My best hope would be that they'd just fire me, send me away. But I know a lot about them and what they do. So I think my dismissal would more likely take the form of someone marching me into the woods along a country road somewhere east of Tiraspol."

Dan finishes his first martini. His second already awaits. Agata's second is empty.

"What happened in the States?"

"I'm a reporter. Was a reporter," she says, nodding to the bartender for a third. "I wrote an article, actually three articles in a series, about a pharmaceutical company that connived to rig pricing. I won a Scripps-Howard Award for it, and a Robert F. Kennedy, and a Sigma Delta Chi. I was nominated for a Pulitzer."

"Ah, you're that Agata Svendson," Dan says. "I read those articles in the *Times* when they came out. I also recall reading a little article about you in *The Atlantic*."

She smiles at him, but the smile fades and she sits looking down the bar past him for a minute. Slowly, her head sinks forward until her face is in her hands. She stays like that, breathing huskily, until she releases a single audible sob. Presently, she raises her head and wipes angrily at tears with a bar napkin and begins to talk again.

"The thing is, I made a lot of that up. There were areas I just couldn't get to. I knew it was all true, the core of what I was investigating and writing about. They were bad guys. It was just a little beyond my fingertips. I knew that people were getting away with terrible things. I just couldn't get my hands around all the background to demonstrate it.

"There were deadlines. Doors were closing. I was running on anger and despair and caffeine. There were probably a number of reasons. My fiancé had just broken it off. One of my brothers was killed in an accident. My sister went into rehab, lost her kids. I had the feeling that I was somewhere I didn't deserve to be, and that my one opportunity to break a big story and feel like a success, like my dad had been, was vanishing. So I sanded down some quotes, exaggerated a few facts, left out some pertinent information, accidentally lost some of my notes. I hid all this from the two assistants who had been assigned to work with me, although I think one of them had an inkling. I faked some emails, phone calls. Essentially, I told only part of the story. My editors didn't know."

She goes still again, studying the rows of bottles for several minutes, Dan signals to the bartender and asks for more bread. It is brought, a row of crusty slices on a plate, along with some olives and soft cheese. Agata bites a piece of bread. She chews for a minute and then continues.

"But I was told by Alvaro that there is a file in the possession of a lawyer in D.C. which, if released, would start an investigation. The prizes would be stripped. It would be a big scandal. I would never work again. My twenty-year career over. My colleagues would all lose their jobs, and their careers, too. We'd be waiting tables the rest of our lives. Who knows, Harvard would probably even pull my degree. But that's not the worst of it."

Dan gives her time to re-gather. They sit in silence. His hands lay clasped on the bar. She looks everywhere but at him. She begins to talk again.

"You see, that whole incident was compounded by another. Based on that article, the FBI investigated the president of the drug company and all the angles I wrote about. They did their own investigation, of course. They only asked me for names of contacts. But the article had caused a public outcry, fired up congressional hearings, that sort of thing, so there was momentum behind it.

"The upshot was that the company president and two other people went to prison. Investors lost millions, some upstanding people, but also some not so much. The drugs were pulled from the market, so any good they were doing was lost for the patients. Everyone was suing everyone."

Dan nods. "I can imagine," he says.

"I watched the whole thing unfold, biting my nails until they bled," Agata says. "Those people weren't convicted on the basis of my word. Nothing from my article was presented in court as evidence. In fact, in *voir dire* they asked the jury if they had read the article or heard about it. Jurors who had were disqualified.

"I didn't send those people to prison. They did that themselves. Nevertheless, I couldn't help but feel that the article I wrote was hanging over the whole thing like a cloud. It was the flash-point. And I know other people were feeling that way, too. Immediately after their sentencing I received the first death threat. Then another and another. There was no question that some of the people who lost out had shady ties, and there were some real hot-heads. That's part of what I had written about."

The group of Russian businessmen stand and begin to move toward the door of the hotel's bar. They're still chatting and barking laughs. They pass behind Dan and Agata.

"Do you understand what they're talking about," she whispers to him.

He nods. "The one with the beard got married a few weeks ago. They were joking about flight attendants. Mostly they're lamenting. Each in his own way. Grief and humor."

After the men have exited, the room is very quiet except for a television which plays quietly at the far end of the bar, watched by the man who passed them earlier, now the only other patron. The man looks repeatedly from his phone to the television and back, slowly, sadly. On the television a game show shimmers.

"The FBI brought me in again but this time they talked to me about protection," Agata says. "Can you imagine me sitting there in some office buried in a building in Manhattan knowing the house of cards I'd built, two guys in suits talking about how best to protect me from some thug who deserved to go to prison but who thought his problems were caused by me? By my lies. I went to the bathroom and was sick.

"I told them I would quietly leave New York and go live with my aunt Frida in Copenhagen for a while. The FBI got me an extended visa so I didn't have to come back in three months. Frida is my dad's older sister. Wonderful, generous lady. She doesn't have two cents to rub together, lives in an old apartment out near Christianshavn. She's partially blind, plays the piano beautifully. She didn't know what was wrong or why I was there. But she took care of me."

Dan nods. "People emerge like that sometimes when we most need them," he says. "It's happened for me a few times. But maybe not often enough."

Agata smiles at him. She sips to the olive and touches it with her tongue. "I had a breakdown," she says softly after another pause. "The shame I contained was worse than the fear of dying. I didn't eat, couldn't sleep. I walked around in the night rain like a crazy person with the church bells ringing everywhere, was brought home by the police a couple of times. I eventually woke up in a hospital."

She tips the glass and eats the olive.

"After that, I began to bounce back a little, started trying to make plans to go back to the States and make things right somehow. I didn't know how that was going to work, but I wanted to make it happen. I read a lot, researched a lot of similar scandals and how the people came through them, made a mountain of notes. In a way, that was an odd sort of therapy. Made me feel like I wasn't the only one who'd made a mistake like that. I had a sense that I was getting somewhere, getting better. There had to be a light at the end of a tunnel which I couldn't yet see."

She sets her glass back on the bar and stretches her arms, eyes closed, and swivels her shoulders in a couple of slight shrugs to release something.

"Then one day, this guy who called himself Mr. Tranchard showed up. You're the only person I've told about all this," she says. "I don't know why."

They sit together for several minutes. Each pursues paths of private thought. After a while, Dan clears his throat. "What do we do next?" he asks. This brings no response from Agata. Dan reaches and places a hand on her shoulder for a moment. She shudders, whether in appreciation or revulsion or release he cannot discern.

"We need sleep," he says. "we're too exhausted to think." He stands from his stool and lifts his little knapsack and his coat. She follows suit.

"One other thing," she says. "Tranchard called me when we were in Rome. He said they got your bag from the place you stayed in Valencia. The hostel found a number in a notebook that was in the bag and sent a message that you'd left it. Apparently, that was Tranchard's number. I guess someone went to the hostel in Valencia and extracted the bag from them, by hook or by crook. My guess it was Franco. So they have your phone and notebooks."

Dan slowly shrugs.

Agata also says, "When I was researching you, I learned about your wife and daughter in Paris. I didn't give that information to Alvaro. I figured it was none of his business. But from what Tranchard said, their names and addresses were in your bag, in your notebooks, in your phone. Tranchard said they were going to track them down in Paris, just in case. He said just in case there's any unpleasantness."

CHAPTER 22

DUBROVNIK
10 November, Friday

In the morning, they meet in the lobby. She says, "I finally slept."

She wears the black coat, the maroon scarf, the beret. Dan withdraws twenty-nine hundred and eighty kuna from a bank machine in the lobby. The money is still flowing, at least for the moment. "I feel like walking a little," he says.

They head east over the crest of the hill toward the shore and the yacht harbor, where the neighborhood still sleeps. A few cats come out to watch them; swallows circle treetops, stray gulls crying in a light grey sky. The morning ferry from Korčula silently enters the harbor. Scents of juniper and seawater hang damply, a faint tang of marine diesel as they descend the hill.

As they walk, they speak a little. "I have to get out of here," Dan says. "Whoever has been following us has now seen us together. The guy with the black mustache. The cash-flow is history after today, I think. I need to keep from getting arrested. I just need to figure out how."

In a café by the harbor, they take their coffees to a table by a side wall below a large bulletin board covered with pinned notices and ads tending toward maritime concerns, desires and ambitions. Dan reads the collection of personal notices and help ads. "Maybe there's a boat going somewhere right now which needs crew," he says.

Agata draws her phone from a coat pocket. "I guess I'll look for flights out of here," she says. "I was thinking last night I might go to London. I have some friends there. I can sort of vanish. I just don't think I'm ready for New York yet." She works on that search for a couple of minutes. Dan continues to study the notices on the board.

Dan stands and reaches to a card from which dangle several slips with telephone numbers. Above the text of the card is a photo of a motorcycle. He asks to borrow Agata's phone. He dials the number and talks in Croatian to someone for several minutes. At the conclusion of the conversation, he says in English, "Thank you. I'm across the street in the café. I'll be right there," and then another sentence in Croatian.

Agata asks, "What did you find?"

Dan says, "I may be out of Dubrovnik in an hour."

Across the street, they enter a boatyard where yachts rest in cradles amid piles of stripped gear and hardware, masts on sawhorses, spaghetti coils of rigging wire and halyards. The whine of sanders and drills vibrates the yard, and the still air stinks of paint and hot gel-coat, sounds and scents familiar to Dan. He speaks to a woman in the office and she directs him toward a young man under a boat at the far end. He wears once-white overalls and holed leather gloves. He is blue-haired. When he removes his goggles and facemask, they leave pale raccoon shapes on his face, his freckles and blonde hair thoroughly stained blue with bottom-paint dust.

The young man leads them through the yard gate and to a small row of parking spaces along the street and to a motorcycle. On the low windshield, a cardboard sign announces that it is for sale: *za prodaju*.

Dan straddles the motorcycle and examines the dials. The young man hands him a key. Dan starts the machine and lets it warm for a minute. Its low rumble echoes off the fronts of the restaurants and shops opposite. The owner's black full-face helmet dangles by its chin strap from the left handlebar grip.

Dan removes the cardboard sign and hands it to Agata. She and the young man stand together by the fence as Dan drives up the street, disappears for a minute, during which they can still hear the soft rise and fall of the bike's engine, a few gearshifts, and then Dan returns.

He re-parks the motorcycle and climbs off. It is a Ducati ST4S Desmoquattro, a low-cut touring bike made for distance. It has panniers. The motorcycle is silver, a darker shade than Agata's suitcase. It is about fifteen years old, its mileage reasonable for its age. The paint is still clear, even over the tank. Dan inspects the sides for dents indicating it's been dropped. He sights along the frame for straightness. He runs his palms around the engine and crankcase feeling for drips. He inspects the tires. Dan and the young man talk for several minutes. Agata waits nearby still holding the sign like a talisman. Dan makes an offer somewhat less than the twelve-thousand kuna asking price. The young man looks glum.

Dan says, "I can give you what you ask, but it will need to be partly in kuna and partly in Euros." The young man brightens and agrees. "One more thing," Dan says. "If you leave the license plate on it, fill it with gas, and throw in the helmet, I'll give you an extra five hundred kuna."

They shake hands, leaving Dan's palm stained slightly blue. They agree to meet again in an hour. On the gentle uphill walk back to the hotel, she asks, "Where are you going to go?"

137

"I don't know."

"Don't know or won't say?"

"This is a tenuous tack I'm taking. The bike won't be registered to me. It's Friday, and I'd like the head start of the weekend. I could find the office and wait in line to register it, but who knows how long all that would take, plus it would immediately come up on public records, plus they may ask to see a driver's license, which I don't have. Lack of registration and insurance may be a problem crossing borders. I'll have the title and a bill of sale and some excuses. Or I should be able to get away with the story that I borrowed it from a friend. We're on an isolated tip of the country. An island, really."

They continue walking in silence for a while. Then Dan continues, "I can't go far in any direction without coming to Bosnia or Montenegro, and from Bosnia the only exit eastward is through Serbia. Or I could put the bike on a ferry and try to go further up the coast to Rijeka or whatever and then ride toward Slovenia and Austria. Or I could go back to Italy on the same boat we came over on. Either way would be heading into the EU. The driver's license issue gets thornier the further west I go, also. South or east seems like the best option. Toward the ancient lands. I suppose I could ditch the motorcycle somewhere."

"If you were just going to get on a ferry and then walk away, I don't think you would buy a motorcycle," she says.

"Maybe. Then again, I've always wanted one of these. Maybe I'll give this to my daughter instead of a scooter."

"I'm scared," Agata says lowly. "I'm scared for me. And I'm scared for you. I have to tell you that for the last however long it's been, you were there, sort of like a companion. I felt that at least there was someone out there on the same crazy path as me, not far away. Now I'll be alone again."

At the hotel they part for their rooms. Dan packs his knapsack. On a sheet of hotel stationery, he writes a bill of sale for the motorcycle, including the disposition of the payment in kuna and Euros. He uses the name Alvaro Rodriguez. He does not mention the license plate. He takes the document to the front desk and asks them to make a copy. He checks out of the hotel and then with his knapsack walks alone back down to the boatyard facing the harbor and completes the sale. The young man goes to a shed and comes back with a second black helmet. "It's my wife's," he says, dusting it off, "but she always hated this thing. Should fit your friend, if you want it."

Dan rides slowly toward the old city, and then turns onto Pavla II; it runs along the harbor's edge on the east under the sterns of the big power yachts and the precipice-like hull of a moored cruise ship. From here, he climbs onto the highway headed north, turning immediately onto the asymmetrical Franjo Tudman suspension bridge. He accelerates, getting a feel for the Ducati, the shared posture of machine and rider. It warms and roars under him.

He only rides a few kilometers before circling back the way he came. This takes ten minutes. He turns back onto the peninsula and to the hotel. He comes into the lobby as Agata is checking out.

"I didn't know if you were coming back," she says.

"We didn't say goodbye," he says. He studies her. "Are you okay?"

"I called the place where I was originally going to stay last night. I wanted to let the lady know that I had to leave early but that the money was on the counter. She told me someone broke in last night, middle of the night. She came out of her apartment in her nightgown. He was rifling through my room.

139

He demanded to know where I had gone, but of course she didn't even know I wasn't there. The police told her they have no idea who he was. She said the police want to ask me some questions, also. I didn't tell her where I was."

"Do you think it was Franco?"

"Undoubtedly. She said he was bald. He's out there right now, not far away. They're looking for me. I can't go to the airport. I don't know what to do."

They stand there for a minute each looking at the other. She has the black coat wrapped tight as armor, hands in pockets. Her face is squared up again, eyes level and forceful, the way he saw her when she was coming down the hill in Cuenca. Her chin is raised, whether to him or the world is unclear.

Then he says, "You'll have to leave the suitcase. But there's room in the panniers for some of your stuff. And a helmet's in there that might be your size."

CHAPTER 23

DUBROVNIK

10 November, Friday

It has been four hours since Dan spotted the advertisement for the motorcycle on the café bulletin board. In the hotel's parking lot, they portion Agata's clothing from the suitcase to the hard-sided panniers. There is space for a couple pairs of jeans, rolled, two or three shirts, underwear, a sweater, a handful of scarves, the other pair of boots, the copy of *Agnes Grey*, a small bag of toiletries.

From the bottom of the suitcase she pulls a black plastic tube about fifty centimeters in length and twelve centimeters in diameter. Screw-down caps with gaskets seal the ends. She carefully places it into the pannier alongside her clothing. She tests the lid of the pannier. Though well-stuffed, it closes and latches. They glance at each other.

"I won't need this anymore," Agata says, lifting the yellow raincoat. "Too bad. It's nice. Not cheap, but they paid for it. I bought it to make it easier for you to spot me in crowds. That was Henri's suggestion. I dyed my hair red for the same reason. But that I think I'll keep."

Dan starts the bike, and Agata clambers on behind him and finds the footpegs with her booted feet. They ride together over the crest of the hill and past the upper gate of the ancient city. She clings tightly, arms vise-like around his ribcage. She is rigid on the seat, does not lean when they corner at first and then leans too much.

Dan takes it slowly to give her time. He circles back along the skirt of the ridge above the city, under the tramway towers. The sky to the west has opened wrists of sunlight above the sea, which gleams like stone.

He enters highway D8 aiming south and accelerates. The big bike rolls effortlessly up through the solid clicks of its gears. He touches 80 kph which to Agata apparently feels like the speed of sound. She shrieks once against the wind.

"You're pushing too hard against the back of my helmet," Dan yells.

"What?"

He flips up his visor and calls over his shoulder to her, "Settle back and relax."

The speed limit on this stretch is 110 kph. Dan gradually lifts the bike to a little less than that. There is no hurry. The objective is to avoid attracting attention.

They circle the bay below and west of the dry spine of the ridge arching into Bosnia above. They cross under the airport, after which most of the midday traffic dissipates, and along the broadening shelf above the ocean, a patchwork of fallow farm-land and scrub. Here some breeze moves sideways off the water, but the motorcycle is very stable. Dan passes a pair of trucks on the slow uphill and settles in through the gentle sway of the high-way. They enter a low forest smelling of sap and sawn wood and smoke, occasional cypresses, marshy ponds in pockets.

Within a few minutes they are in sight of the border station for Montenegro. Dan slows, letting the engine take down their momentum, downshifting. He calls back to Agata, "Showtime."

One lane is closed. There is a short line – three semis, a panel van full of vegetables, a couple of cars. Flanking guards armed with automatic rifles watch them sleepily, pacing the side-walks under the canopies. An agent carrying a tablet compu-ter waves Dan forward. He wears a tight-fitting hat above his Mediterranean peasant face; the cap, like his breast pocket, sports the badge of the country, a black two-headed eagle on an iron-red field. He takes their passports and flips them open.

"Where are you going?"

"Kotor."

"For how long?"

Dan listens to the man's blurred-accent border-English, then imitates. "We're just going down for dinner. Fine day for a ride. If she likes it, we'll come back tomorrow. If not, we'll be back tonight. You know how it is."

"You're from Spain?"

Dan nods. "But I grew up not far from here. In Metković."

The agent looks at Dan for a moment, then suddenly opens two or three buttons on his shirt and spreads it, reveal-ing an NK Neretva emblem on his t-shirt underneath. He grins and Dan gives him a thumbs-up. The guard hands back their passports and waves them through with one hand, re-buttoning his shirt with the other.

"What was that about?" Agata asks over his shoulder.

"Football."

They ride gradually downhill toward the bay and Herceg Novi with its fragmentary fortress and sleepy streets. They curve along the shore of the bay, past rows of beach houses, small restau-rants, low apartments, shops, residue of summertime commerce.

The sun has emerged and the water glints. As they round old stone walls and ancient little buildings fronting the bay, every few seconds opens a new view. Agata's grip has loosened. She rides now with her hands on his hips, her face turned outward to the water, the unfolding drama of mountain and fjord and old architecture, molded into the slow warmth between them, the rumble of the machine between their legs carrying them in graceful sweeping curves.

They make the long loop around the inner edge of the waterway and start south again past Risan with its single Venetian church spire and low cavalcade of white stone buildings facing beach cafés. Dan points up the ridge to the fortifications on the hill and calls, "Carine, Roman site, some good mosaics, an Illyrian acropolis."

But Agata says, "What? Goodness sakes Iberian populace?" They share a quick laugh over the wind.

Dan points out Our Lady of the Rocks as the knobbed island passes, but does not try to yell to her. By the time they arrive in Kotor the sun has dropped below the ridge to the southwest. If cruise ships came today, they have left, and the town belongs again to its own.

They motor across the bridge over the half-dried inlet and turn into a section of the plaza before the main gate into the city where scores of scooters and a few other motorcycles park under palm trees. Dan slides under a pair of trees at the end of a line of vehicles and backs the motorcycle in. He unclips the panniers and carrying these, they walk the striped pavements through the arched and heavy-columned Sea Gate in the city walls and up into the labyrinth of cobblestone streets.

Midweek strollers out before dinner amble the streets in groups of twos, threes, half-dozens. Dan and Agata make a slow meandering circuit of the little triangular town in the soft twilight. Dan points out a few things he remembers: St. Tryphon's Cathedral, baroque-faced Pima Palace, the blocky little clock tower, ancient cisterns built into walls, limbs of fortifications named after St. John rising floodlit here and there. The doors of St. Luke's stand open for evening Mass.

They spot a guesthouse with a diminutive sign on a sliver of side street. The man who comes to their ring of the bell is birdlike, mustachioed, dragging a trail of pipe tobacco, with a sharkskin vest and a sweep of snowy hair. Dan asks for a room with two beds. The man leads them up endless creaking wooden steps to a garret.

In the room, they lock the door and open the plastic tube. They are both breathless.

He sights down it. He slides two fingers into the tube and slowly draws out a rolled item. He spreads the item across the bed and removes a sheet of tissue paper which covers it top to bottom.

The painting's overtones are blue, with fringes of ochre and a creamy center; reclining and seated nude figures, a child, a vague forest scene. It has been pulled from its stretcher. Frayed tack holes line the edges of the canvas. The bare edges of the canvas are softly sepia-toned, sand-colored. The painting is almost square, the length of a forearm. It rises from the mattress as if alive, holding a slight curve from being rolled.

Dan lifts it carefully by its edges and examines the underside, some illegible markings, lays it back on the bed.

Dan says, "I seem to remember there was also a Léger, a Modigliani, something else. A Picasso, I believe. Another one, too."

"A Braque. That was the other one," Agata says. "Alvaro was the latest in a string of owners of this one. Possessors. Henri said he killed a guy for it, but Henri tends to exaggerate. Then again, that could be the case with this. It's something worth killing for, if you're the killing type. A hundred million Euros. That's what they said the paintings were worth at the time they were taken."

145

They both sit for a long time with their elbows on their knees, studying.

Later, over dinner at a table on the cobbled sidewalk facing a segment of the old city wall, Agata says, "Quite a day, this one." Gas torchieres flutter. At other tables, a few diners clink silver and glassware. They've almost finished one bottle of wine and have ordered another. "I feel like I'm getting somewhere. Not sure where, though. How am I doing at riding a motorcycle?"

"You're a natural."

"My older brother had a motorcycle. He took me for rides around New Haven a few times. He was always angry and reckless. He later died."

"On a motorcycle?"

"No, on a mechanical bull in a cowboy bar in Buffalo one January."

She takes another drink and goes on.

"He was very drunk. Runs in my family. Killed two uncles and my grandmother, also. And my mother."

"When?"

"My mother?"

"No, when did your brother die?"

"More than ten years ago. Shortly before I took the job with the *Times*. I always wanted him to see me as worthy of his love, but he was gone before my imagination bore fruit. I mostly remember him as a little girl remembers things, being carried around on his shoulders, him holding my hand by the lake in the park, him teaching me about hamsters. Being proud of him. He was six years older than I was."

Dan pours a little more wine before responding. "Makes me think of my brother."

"A drunk?"

"No, a priest. The paradox of the family. He soared through the diocese of Quebec, had a parish of his own, loved by so many people. But then problems started to show up. He was moved around for a couple years and then eventually excised altogether. Defrocked, I think. I was never clear on the details. He lives in Toronto now and runs a homeless shelter. He has HIV."

Agata pauses, seems to consider her next words.

"What did you do? If you want to tell me. I know only the bare outlines."

He clears his throat and sips some wine. "I was teaching at the University of Quebec. Romance languages, Russian, a comparative lit class. But I was also moonlighting doing some consulting work for the government, for CSIS, the intelligence service. Translation work. I left the University. Some cutbacks, a little protest scandal. Then an opportunity came up to work full-time for CSIS.

"I was assigned to all the cases with language difficulties. There was a case with a Brazilian man in Vancouver who didn't speak English or French. I handled his interviews in Portuguese. A thug, a drug dealer. He murdered another Brazilian man along with his wife and children. Tortured them, shot them, stuffed them in a camper van and then set the van on fire. A brutal revenge killing. The other man had testified against him. We had evidence, DNA and everything else. We had witnesses. Plus, he had all but admitted it.

"There were rounds of depositions, both early in the process and later after he had been in jail for a while awaiting trial. I was the principal translator all the way through. The depositions were recorded, of course, but I translated on the spot for the lawyers and later wrote the transcripts from the recordings. The transcripts are supposed to be reviewed, but I stamped them as approved, which I had the authority to do since I was a senior case manager. That was my first mistake."

The waiter brings dinner. They eat in silence. The torchieres flutter. Nearby conversations meander. A woman walking a bicycle comes slowly along the curving street. All sounds reflect to them stonily off the wall.

Dan resumes talking after each has taken several bites. "Canada has had a long-standing problem with trials taking too long and defendants getting off because time runs out. We were nearing the deadline on this guy. That's when I made my second mistake. I'm not sure why I did it. I was exhausted and angry. Angelique had left for France with my daughter two weeks earlier. I hadn't slept in a long time. I was living in a hotel room not far from Stanley Park. It rained constantly. I hit one of my low points. Suicide versus dull fury. Not sure if it was recklessness, or righteousness, or maybe some blurry place between those two.

"I altered the transcripts a little to make it sound like he had personal knowledge of a second murder. I knew this would tip the balance toward giving the court reason to grant a motion to hold onto him longer. He deserved to die, I thought, which I'd never felt about anyone before. I was not my controlled self. Some other self."

Agata pours more wine for them both. "That's something we share. Multiple selves. Who was it, Walt Whitman, I think, who said, *I am large and contain multitudes?*"

Dan nods. "*Do I contradict myself? Very well then, I contradict myself.* And Emerson said, *Consistency is the hobgoblin of little minds.* So we must be grandly brilliant." He smiles. They raise their glasses.

"By altered," Dan continues, "I mean I changed the inflections of some words and phrases the guy used. Brazilian

148

Portuguese differs from standard in a variety of ways. Gerunds, modifiers, adverbs, sentence length, colloquial expressions. In Lisbon, an *apelido* is someone's last name; in Rio, it's just a nickname. Things like that can add up. A serious turn of phrase in Portugal may be a joke in Brazil.

"We had tapes of this guy slurring and swearing and barking at us. But I cleaned up what he said, so to speak, and applied some meanings to things that should not have been assumed. Later, I went back and made a couple of tweaks to the first set of transcripts so they would line up. That was the biggest mistake, of course. While the first embellishment episode was unprofessional and immoral, grey-area illegal, going back and altering the first set of transcripts was downright stupid because the lawyers already had those."

Agata shakes her head slowly, watching Dan. "We've walked some of the same pathways," she says softly. Her eyes shine in the light from the torch flames.

Dan nods. "Bottom line, it worked. At first. He was held over and convicted. He appealed. Then a new lawyer, a sharper one, asked for all the transcripts and the tapes and found the differences. CSIS opened an internal investigation and questioned me about it. I had a mini breakdown during this and took a leave of absence. Some of my colleagues were trying to protect me, others not so much. A month later a warrant was issued for my arrest, but that was when I was on a sailboat in the middle of the Atlantic bound for France."

The two sit in silence for a while, eating. Each looks in different directions, Dan at the wall and Agata at her plate. Then they look at each other again. Dan raises his eyebrows.

He says, "So here I am seven years later in a good restaurant under an old fortress on a gorgeous evening in Kotor. Some would say I'm doing fine. But things are not fine. Something is afoot within me. A vortex of circumstances is closing in."

He pauses, looking to his food as if for clues. "Before, I couldn't leave Europe, Paris, Angelique, Gennie. They were my magnet. I've ambled about, but always in vague orbit around my wife and daughter."

Laughter bursts from a group sharing stories at a nearby table. It rings in the alley for a moment. Dan and Agata glance to them, then back to their meals.

Dan continues more in rumination than conversation, "I'm an expatriate. There are those who stay home and those who leave home. I leave. I wander with purpose. Landscapes and languages; always, the next place beckons. This has been my hunger and joy. I never knew why."

He stops and sets down his fork. "But now I'm exhausted. In Madrid, after I got the job of following you, I briefly thought I'd rediscovered that bliss of motion, of simply being elsewhere, not small Canada. But it's gone. I think this time for good. Maybe now my polarity has finally begun to shift. The magnet's power has diminished. The wind has calmed."

Agata does not reply to this. She sits holding her spoon thoughtfully.

"What are you going to do?" he asks presently.

"I don't know yet. I don't think I'm quite to the point that you are."

As they walk back to their lodging, a million small reflections rise from the ripples on the bay. In the guesthouse, the man with the pipe emerges from a kitchen. He offers them tea. Dan chats with him for several minutes while Agata stands nearby looking at a carved chestnut mantlepiece.

In their room, Dan says to Agata, "He's Albanian. He used to go visit his daughter in Tirana every weekend. But he says it's becoming too difficult and time-consuming at the border on the road from Podgorica to Shkodër. Long lines, endless checks. They're going through every vehicle with a fine comb."

Later, they lie in their separated beds but not far apart in the darkness under the timbered vaulting. Outside in the narrow alley, a few echoing voices pass and fade. The room smells lightly of dust and rust and medieval stonework and lemons.

After a while, Dan says, "I shouldn't have gone into all of that at dinner."

There is a period of silence. Two humans lie breathing.

Then Agata says, "And that you would fret like that is another way we're similar."

CHAPTER 24

KOTOR

11 November, Saturday

They wake early. The little room is already warm from sunshine on the slate roof. They take turns showering in the crooked and tilting bath down the stairs from their room, each ascending back to the bedroom in their towels leaving wet footprints on the old steps.

"I think we're safe for the time being," Dan says. "Let's take a little time."

They walk up the zigzag pathway along Kotor's fortification walls, ascending the ridge toward the remnants of the castle. Crowds thin. They stop to look at the view, the walled town in its nook between the rivers and the cup of the bay, a ship at the wharf and another anchored a half-kilometer out of the harbor. The sun and the climb have warmed them and they take off their jackets.

They walk slowly back down into town. But by the time they are again in the shadowy streets they are chilled. On their way back to the guesthouse they pass a clothing shop with male and female mannequins wearing coats displayed in the windows along with signs offering pre-Christmas discounts. They go inside. They each buy a new jacket. Agata replaces her long woolen coat which is thin and flaps in the wind on the bike with a slim shorter jacket made of black lambskin. Dan replaces his cotton jacket with a coat slightly longer with a zipping collar and made of heavy weather-resistant twill, also black. They buy gloves.

At the guesthouse, Agata gives her wool coat to the proprietor for his wife, but he tries it on and it fits him well.

There is an old computer on a side table in the hotel. When they return, Agata sits at it and opens her email. Dan is chatting with the guesthouse's Albanian owner when Agata says, "Dan," in a voice like breaking glass.

She points to an email. Dan reads it over her shoulder. "*We know you're in Kotor.*"

Agata turns to Dan and raises her hands. "How could they possibly know?"

Dan studies the email. "It doesn't say who sent it." He points to the address lines of the email. "Could have been anybody."

In their room, he paces. Finally, he sits on the bed.

"They're tracking us somehow. Our phones haven't been on. Either they're more sophisticated than I thought and the phones don't need to be on. Or they have some other way. You don't have a device implanted under your skin, do you?"

Agata's jaw is set the way he has seen it in the past.

"Empty your purse," Dan says. "Your toiletries bag, too."

She dumps these onto the bed and Dan runs his fingers through the assortment of items. He examines the small collection of squeeze tubes and jars. "Not as if I would know what to look for anyway," he says. "Let me see your boots."

He examines these also, pulls out the insoles, taps at the heels. "Maybe we should just get rid of all of it."

"I'll just go," she says. "I'll get a ride back to Dubrovnik somehow and then fly somewhere. I won't take you down with me."

"Notice they said Kotor, not Montenegro. So it wasn't crossing the border. I guess there could be security cameras around here. Some sort of face recognition. No idea how they could tap into that. MI-6 maybe. The CIA. The Kremlin maybe. Not some jackass gangsters."

She watches his demeanor. He sorts possibilities.

"They gave you that phone, right?" he says. "I have to think it's the phones. They installed some sort of parental tracking application on yours, mine or both, and we can't see them. The phones don't have to be used for them to be located within cells."

He takes his phone out of the pannier and turns it on. "Do you have anything on yours that you want to save?" he asks.

They go downstairs again and he creates a new email account with a general web service. From his phone he tries to send a text containing the photos he has taken to his new email address, and it works, maybe because it's not a phone number. He texts himself the numbers from the contact list, too. Then he turns the phone off.

She says, "There's nothing on here that I want except Henri's contact info and a photo of my Aunt Frida." She texts those to his new address and then turns off her phone.

"Let's get rid of these now," Dan says.

They descend through the town, through the Sea Gate. Now, neither of them walk gently. They look around, peer into the faces of people on the streets. Their shoulders hunch. They cross the highway to the harbor quay.

"Are we going to throw them into the water?" Agata asks.

"I'm thinking more along the lines of misdirection," Dan says.

The large cruise ship that they saw from high on the ridge is moored at the quay. Streams of passengers meander back to the ship and to the shuttle boats ferrying passengers to the other ship anchored in the harbor. The gate to the pier is open and guards are inattentive. Dan and Agata pass through with a large group of passengers. "Your ship is pretty," Dan says to an old couple walking near them toward the moored vessel. "Where are you headed next?"

"We just came from Corfu. We're going to Venice," the man says.

At the midpoint of the pier, stacks of provisions on pallets await loading onto the ship. A worker on the dock waits for the forklift to emerge from the cargo ramp again. His back is to Dan and he stares at something in the water between ship and quay. The cargo is mixed: bottled water, cartons of oranges and lemons, lettuce, paper goods, cases of wine, cases of liquor.

"Give me your phone. Now go distract the guard."

"How am I supposed to do that?"

"He's smoking. Ask him for a cigarette and a light."

Dan stands near the straggling crowds, takes out his phone as if capturing a photo of the blunt bow of the ship rising above them with its heavy hawsers draping toward the bollards. He watches Agata.

She talks to the man, who evidently does not speak English because Dan then sees Agata pantomime smoking and tilting her head at the guard with a pleading expression. The guard pulls a pack of cigarettes from a coat pocket and taps one out for her, digs in another pocket for a lighter. He lights her cigarette, grins and hands her the lighter with a shrug.

Dan steps to a nearby pallet. It is loaded with bundles of toilet paper and wrapped in heavy plastic sheeting. Dan feels the weight of the plastic in a pinch between fingers, tries to tear at it, and then simply pokes a finger through multiple layers and into the core of a roll of toilet paper. He takes both phones from his pocket and stuffs them, twisting, one at a time through the hole and into the core of the toilet paper roll. He strolls back casually with his hands in his pockets.

Agata sees him, smilingly thanks the guard. She rejoins Dan with her cigarette, coughing.

"The phones are on their way to Venice," Dan says. "Now let's get out of this town."

CHAPTER 25

KOTOR
11 November, Saturday

With the panniers re-clipped to the Ducati, they motor slowly along the M-2 as it parallels the city walls to the south. They pass a row of vendor stalls. Simultaneously, they both see a man walking quickly past the other direction: black hair, mustache, sunglasses, windbreaker. The man swivels to watch the motorcycle with its two riders as they pass.

Agata grips Dan. After they have advanced a block, she leans forward and says over his shoulder, "Is that the guy we saw at the bar in Dubrovnik?" Dan nods.

He angles into Škaljari at the tip of the bay. But instead of proceeding with the flow of traffic into the 1.5-kilometer Tunel Vrmac, he turns onto quiet, sinuous R-22, the old road, which ascends through a sequence of tight switchbacks over a low pass. They lean into the bends. On a crumbling retaining wall encircling a narrow curve, graffiti in block letters announces to passers-by, *Ako vjeruješ, bijeg.* Dan gives the wall a thumbs-up.

"What does it mean?" she calls over his shoulder.

He raises his face screen to be more audible. "If you believe, escape."

They cross the pass. The land in the saddle and the mountains rising above: karst and scrub. The land lower: karst and low pine forest, carrying scents of oleander and terebinth and increasing humidity. The old road toward Podgorica branches off, but Dan continues along R-22 as it winds down into broad valleys to the east. They enter a sub-climate cupped by knuckled mountains, its few small farms picturesque with hand-dug wells and goat-cheese-for-sale signs, the tumbled remains of walls made of stones not improbably stacked by Illyrian hands three thousand years ago.

Traffic grows denser as they move south. They are in a line of vehicles rolling smoothly now with headlights coming on as daylight dwindles, past markets and auto dealers, clumps of concrete apartments, strip malls offering salons and small engine repairs, all spread among desiccated copses of holly oak, prickly juniper and Aleppo pine. Bursting in just north of Budva, the Adriatic rises under the remains of the late-autumn sunset. Dan drives carefully but quickly. He passes cars occasionally with a quick twist of the throttle, and Agata grips tightly. They both sit tensely, hunched.

South of Budva, Dan pulls into a rustic beach café with a hedge-screened fence protecting the carpark and slips into a motorcycle-sized space near steps to the beach.

The terrace of the restaurant is still open, though they have it to themselves and the waiter wears a puffy down jacket over her apron. Infrared heaters glow along the edge of the canopy. The ocean is dark, but Dan points out the shape of Mogren fortress on the peninsula and the lighted outline of Sveti Nikola island.

Agata muses over her tumbler of wine. "So do you think we're finally free of them? Maybe?"

Dan considers this for a full minute. He looks up at her. "No."

They eat and watch the sea. A boat travels by in the darkness a kilometer out, just a line of mast-head light, a wavering gem of green starboard running lamp and a glow from the galley. Agata watches Dan watching the boat. "If you had a sailboat," she says, "you could sail us away from here."

Dan quotes a line from the Ferrante novel he finished a day earlier: "*In fairy tales one does as one wants. In reality one does what one can.*"

"I'm curious. Do you have a personal code that you live by? You know, some sort of private creed?"

"Do I seem that rigid?"

"Not at all. That's why I thought you might."

Dan shrugs. "Yes, I suppose. I used to recite: Make yourself useful. Mind your manners. Talk enough, but not too much. Build upon the good that you find. Clean up after yourself." He taps a finger on the tabletop with each point.

Agata nods. "That sounds very much like you."

Dinner finished, they remount the motorcycle.

Agata says, "I feel like Steve McQueen. Can we jump over a fence or something?" She had finished off most of their bottle of wine. They pull quietly onto the highway and continue south along the coast. Headlights stream in both directions on the brusque little road.

Dan points out the 11th-century monastery of Praskvica, a demure ghost in a veil of trees. He points out the glowing resort island of Sveti Stefan with its gated causeway funneling from unctuous beaches lit for the evening, though vacant. They ride together close in the dark and the hum of old quiet power over the dark ridge and down into the outskirts of Bar.

CHAPTER 26

BAR

11 November, Saturday

Dan brings Agata to the harbor and the fishing marina. They walk the docks in the dark, boats clanging around them, the smells of frying fish and potatoes swelling from galleys, gulls complaining about nighthawks. Dan explains to Agata that here he may find people he knew, maybe people who would put them up for a night or two, hide the motorcycle somewhere.

A crossroad, Bar offers options. They could still aim back through the Sozina Tunnel to Podgorica and from there branch out elsewhere. They could take a ferry back to Italy, to Ancona or Brindisi or Bari. They could try the border crossing into Albania at Sukobin. But just as Dan is running through this list, they encounter a man coming up a dock from a line of fishing boats moored sterns to quay.

"Bilo," Dan says.

"Dan," says the other man. After hugs between the men and introductions, the three cross to the tavern facing the harbor.

Dan and Agata sit with Bilo at a wooden table. They talk over glasses of Smirnoff.

"I have a warm place in my heart for Bar. I landed here during an especially rough patch. It was fishermen like Bilo here who took me in. I knew nothing about fishing and the fishing life."

"But he could stand solid on a deck in steep seas, he understood wind and rain, he never got sick, he had a get-up-and-go personality, he didn't take shit from anyone." The man called Bilo says this to Agata in heavily-accented English.

Dan says, "At that moment, this was probably four years ago or so, I had some sort of mysterious determination. I suppose the low point of my neurosis. But I blended myself in. The fishermen found me useful and not overly irritating. I was mildly amusing."

"This guy," Bilo says gesturing to Dan, "saved my ass many times that year. Most reliable crew I ever had. I was truly sorry to see you leave for, what was it, Stockholm?"

"You threw a great party for me, as I recall. Or don't recall."

A forest of masts spreads in the dim light beyond in the marina. An occasional scooter passes in the street. In the room with them, patrons sit at a couple of tables, a few more in a row along the bar. Televisions show football, Rotterdam versus Graz, Man U versus Leicester, and a cricket game in India.

"Quit smoking since I saw you last," Bilo says now. "Thirty years of smoking, dropped it just like that."

"I bet Regina was happy about that," Dan says.

"So happy she got pregnant again."

"How many kids do you have now, Bilo?"

"Eight that I know of." He grins at Agata.

Bilo resembles a tree stump on a hillside. He is wider than the chair. His face belies wind and sun and lack of medical care for small injuries and offenses. He shaves occasionally, and not carefully. He could be in his forties or in his seventies. His nose is long and Viking. What remains of his hair is uncut and blonde. It responds in drifting shades to the red and green neon and the blue flutter of televisions.

161

Dan asks, "Is Bar as quiet as it used to be?"

"It's a peaceful place. We get along. We're a very mixed people," he explains to Agata. "Christians, Muslims, Orthodox. Slavs, Croats, Greeks. Everyone has multiple identities. Growing up, I didn't sense any differences between people, just that they celebrated different holidays."

"Are you still trawling for sea bass?" Dan asks.

Bilo nods. "Less money in it year after year, though. Croatia just locked down everything a little tighter. The closer they move to the EU the stricter everything is getting. I used to keep four guys employed. Between the government and the German environmentalists, we're starving.

"Don't get me wrong," he says to Agata, "I'm all for saving the fisheries." Then to Dan again: "Are you back to stay a while? Maybe fish a little again?"

Dan shakes his head. "Just passing through."

"It would be nice to spend time with you. But there's no money anywhere. Both my older sons and my daughter are out of work. I wish I had some view forward. I wish I had the cash to take Regina somewhere for our anniversary. So many years go by."

Dan's elbows rest on the table. His hands form a steeple under his chin. "What would you like to do for Regina?"

"You know that fancy resort on Sveti Stefan up the coast? With the movie stars and tennis stars and so forth? I'd like to take her there for a couple days, let her enjoy the spa and the whole thing. She deserves it. Maybe I do, too."

Dan gazes down into his beer for a minute, then up at Bilo.

"An idea just crossed my mind," he says. "You remember those places just inside the inlet in Velipojë where we used to stop sometimes?"

Bilo laughs and raises his glass for a toast.

Dan continues, "Would you be willing to make a quick run down there, drop us off? And a small piece of cargo."

"What cargo?"

"A motorcycle."

Bilo looks at the pair. "I wouldn't object. It's a tight channel getting in there, but I've done it a few times, as you know. There's a sandbar, but it's doable at high tide. That's across the border, of course. The Albanian Coast Guard has a little cutter stationed in Shëngjin now with three or four crew. But they usually patrol only during the day. We see them sometimes down past Ulcinj. They've stopped a couple people I know, asked to see their licenses. Why do you want to go that way?"

Dan says, "We're heading south. I've heard the borders are tight. Albania has refugee paranoia. They're examining everybody. Our passports may be worthless."

"That's true about the border. It's become a real pain getting to Tirana. Police after you?"

"No, we just need to keep moving. We would pay you," Dan adds.

Bilo nods, doesn't say anything but wears an expression indicating inquiry.

Agata speaks up. "Enough to take your wife on holiday to that resort."

The three of them sit for a minute, all leaning forward onto the table.

"When would you want to go?"

"How's the tide tonight?"

Bilo says, "For you, my friend, just fine."

Fifteen minutes later, Dan coasts the bike slowly down the ramp onto the dock. Its old timbers creak under the Ducati's weight. He turns off the engine and propels the bike forward a few boat lengths under leg power, past coiled lines and striped floats and stacks of crab traps, to the stern of Bilo's boat.

The dock is vacant. Six flood lamps on spaced poles aim down onto the boards, but three are burned out or broken. Only a few lights, the glow of a television, some muted laughter indicate people on some of the trawlers and seiners.

Bilo and a young crewman, a teenager, have started the boat's engines and the hydraulic pumps. By the time Dan gets the motorcycle to the boat, they have swung the arm of the deck crane out over the dock. The young man, disheveled, recently-wakened but bright-eyed, is attaching a sling of nylon straps to the hook at the end of the cable. He smells strongly of youth and unwashed laundry. He and Dan wrap the straps under the motorcycle's frame.

On board, Bilo pulls the crane control slowly and tests the fit of the sling a centimeter or two. Then he lifts the motorcycle off the dock and hoists it over the stern-mounted trawler machinery and brings the bike gently down onto the deck directly behind the pilot-house bulkhead forward of the fish hold.

Dan and the young man scramble aboard. They leave the sling in place and tie the bike to eyebolts in the bulkhead with a length of line taken from a storage box. Then they jump back onto the dock to cast off mooring lines. As Bilo eases the boat away from the dock, they step aboard once more.

Dan stands beside Agata in the dark at the port rail.

"How long will it take to get there?"

"Maybe three hours," he says.

"Where are we going?"

"Velipojë. It's a town just across the border. Sits on an inlet. Small marina. Some beaches. Very sleepy place, especially this time of year."

"What happens if they stop us?"

"They'll send us back, I think. But to be safe why don't you stow the tube down below someplace? Ask the boy if you can stuff it in his locker. No one will dig through that."

Agata does this, and by the time she rejoins Dan and Bilo in the wheelhouse, they have cleared the breakwater and face an empty and shining night sea. The lights of Bar recede behind them. Bilo angles for a channel buoy a half kilometer out and opens a bottle of beer.

The boat picks up a soft Mediterranean swell about a kilometer offshore. A breeze is just stiffening from the west. The sky is clear, but sea haze drapes over the land, blears stars and lights along the coast. Westward, the sky blots with a line of gently advancing rainstorms. Only a quarter moon casts tarnished silver across the swell.

Radar shows little traffic. A small vessel advances up the coast in the dark to the north. A very large vessel, probably a freighter, somewhere out in the Adriatic at the perimeter of the radar's range, heads toward the lonely gap into the Ionian. The trawler's big twin diesels huddle and shudder beneath their feet, tuned to each other. Thin carpet that smells vaguely of fish and maritime mechanical anatomy pads the wheelhouse deck.

Bilo holds the boat close to the coast and lays a straight course down the bay toward the point north of Ulcinj. He sets the autopilot. They are just off the low shelf where the seas begin to steepen shoreward, and the heavy trawler rides comfortably.

Dan steps out of the wheelhouse for a moment and onto the slim bow deck. He stands with a knee braced against the windlass and hands on the railing. He gazes off into the dark. Agata and Bilo watch him from inside.

"He misses this," Bilo says. "The sea is in his blood. Motion is in his blood. Loneliness is in his blood."

Dan reenters the wheelhouse and tunes through marine radio channels, searching for Albanian traffic, maybe comments from the coast guard. He finds Arabic chatter, Greek chatter, recorded weather and sea-state reports in Italian. The three pass an hour in comfortable quiet in the warm wheelhouse. Dan dozes in the helm seat. Bilo cracks an occasional beer. Then he remembers a bottle stowed in a drawer. He pours shots for Agata and himself. The wheelhouse is in complete darkness except for the binnacle, oil and water pressure dials, the numbers on the tuners of the radios and vague glow from the hooded radar screens.

Agata talks sports with Bilo.

"I like to watch unusual events," she says. "I went to the London Olympics. I follow curling."

"In my family, watching sports on TV replaced going to Mass," Bilo says.

"In my family, not going to Mass replaced going to Mass," Agata says.

The young man comes up from the cabins forward and talks with Dan for a few minutes in Montenegrin. Dan points to big greenish smudge crawling across the radar screen, closing on the boat bull's-eyed in the center. Bilo nods.

"Just some squalls coming in," Dan says to Agata. "Typical fall weather. Nothing to worry about. Might get a little bumpier."

"It's good luck," Bilo says. "Gives us some cover. There's a military radar installation on the bluff just south of the point. I'll stay close." He leans to a switch panel and clicks off the boat's running lights just as a gust reaches them with the first spattering of rain on the deck.

The weather wraps the boat and bangs on the windshield. Three or four times the wind rises and roars. Rain thunders sideways. A few taller seas slam the bow, jerking the people in the wheelhouse, sending black spray leeward.

Bilo takes the boat off autopilot and steers by hand for a while, lazily slumped on the helmseat with his drink in the other hand, feathering the heavy boat into the waves. They round the point only a few hundred meters off the breaking waves on the shore. Bilo watches the depth sounder, which as they cross the undersea delta suddenly slides from seventy meters up to twenty meters and then to ten.

Lights of houses on shore are no longer visible. They cross the northerly mouth of the Bojana River and round the square tip of the island. They trace the surf rising against the main mouth of the Bojana just offshore. The seas have become steep and harsh and the boat pitches and wallows plaintively.

Agata, in the light from the radar, looks greenish. She holds the teak rail on the panel in front of them. Dan places a hand on her shoulder and says, "We're getting close." Bilo adds, "We're in Albania now."

They parallel the beach a few hundred meters from the shore still running under no lights. The boat's motion smooths and changes to a slow, metronomic shuffle. The rain lessens. Yellow streetlights and lights in the hotels along the shore emerge and sharpen.

Within a few minutes they have rounded the sandy point of the inlet and turned straight north. Briefly, the waves lift and scoot the heavy boat, and then they level. The vessel motors smoothly in a foaming confusion of squall-stirred sea in the shallows. Ahead, lights appear on docks.

They pass two short concrete piers and a tumbledown timber pier, then pull against a dock sloping upward to a restaurant with windows dark and shining in the rain and on its roof a red-lighted sign depicting crabs. The young crewman is off the boat and running mooring lines before Dan has cleared the rail. Bilo goes to the crane controls. Within two minutes, the motorcycle sits on the dock.

"You should be able to get out," Bilo calls. "I think that gate only locks from the outside."

Agata has taken a wad of cash from her purse and counts out a stack of bills for Bilo. He bends and they kiss on both cheeks. Then she clambers back into the boat and emerges a minute later with the plastic tube embraced.

Dan runs back and shakes Bilo's hand, hugs him.

By the time he has started the motorcycle, the broad, dark shape of his Montenegrin friend has stepped back aboard his boat and the broader, darker shape of the trawler is pulling away from the dock. The boat heads for the light line of risen seas in the mouth of the little estuary and the darkness of open water beyond. Its searchlight blinks on, sweeps the surf to spot the center of the channel and immediately switches off.

Dan drives up the dock and Agata follows on foot at a run. She slips past him and holds open the gate in the chain link fence lined with razor wire as Dan skids through on the steel grating and up the ramp. She climbs on behind Dan, pulls on her helmet and threads her chin strap through its d-rings with one hand, holding the plastic tube tightly to her chest with the other for just a moment, before putting it into the pannier. They motor slowly up through the parking lot past the restaurant. They both stream rain. Their helmets gleam red in the light from the crab sign.

CHAPTER 27

VELIPOJË

12 November, Sunday

It is three in the morning in Velipojë, Albania, population five thousand. The two riders progress up a dirt street that changes to dimpled and pitted pavement, then back again. The tires of the bike splash through long dancing puddles. Dan chooses a road which runs along the edge of the estuary on a raised embankment, headlight glinting off dank stands of trees planted in rows and rush-clogged marsh ponds and a canal.

By the time they find the end of the estuary and cross a bridge over a shallow and clotted river, the rain has lessened and when they have circled back to the southern side of the waterway, the moon has even made brief appearances. They travel ten, fifteen kilometers without encountering another vehicle or seeing anything in motion. Along the road, occasional dark houses emerge, houses with a single porch light or a single light in a back room. They pass a closed gas station. They pass an all-night laundromat with a blue-lit sign. No one is laundering.

Habitations thin further and the road becomes an access to kilometers of dunes. The remaining drizzle stops. On the far side of the sand lie the beach and the sea. The dunes prevent views, but the sense of the sea crosses them, its scent and magnetism. A vacant campground, ticket office and rows of empty caravan pads among skeletal trees crouch on the landward side of the road. Dan drives very slowly. Both of them are soaked, and the wind is frigid. Dan turns west on a sandy track toward the beach.

Ahead, the headlight picks out two rounded moonlit shapes, dense black and grainy. The shapes turn into two domes, each ten meters in diameter, concrete, joined by a low segment of concrete building: Hoxha bunkers. Dan coasts the motorcycle quietly down the last of the road to them.

He stops. Agata climbs off, pulls the plastic tube from the pannier with wet, pale hands. Dan raises the bike on its kick-stands and tests its footing in the sand. They walk around the more southerly of the two domes. Trash and windblown scree clutch at its skirt. A gun slot gapes in the west-facing side. Corroded re-bar protrudes from crumbling walls. The edifice stands black and silver in the moonlight.

The site of a former campfire collects against the seaward wall of the building. Here, little wind circulates. Dunes which have grown around the site over the decades protect the spot. The blackened pit, among stray rocks and chunks of broken concrete, is still damp from the rain.

Dan strikes out in the direction of the sea, a hundred meters away, where a high line of sea-washed debris runs parallel to the meager surf. Agata stands by the dome's wall with her arms wrapped around herself and the tube, shaking. Dan returns a few minutes later with an armload of driftwood pieces. He sets about constructing a fire teepee-style in the blackened pit.

"Do you have that lighter?"

She digs in a coat pocket and produces the lighter given to her by the dock-guard in Kotor. Dan goes to the motorcycle, pulls his notebook from his knapsack and tears out the pages on which he made notes about his marriage. He crumples the pages and stuffs them under the chips and fragments of driftwood in the firepit and lights them.

Agata and Dan stand close to the fire, extending their palms to its flames. The legs of their jeans begin to steam. From down the beach rise occasional surges of low surf and sifting sand and bits of shells in slow outwash.

Once more, Dan goes to the motorcycle and returns this time with both panniers. Agata changes her jeans and socks.

"It'll be light in a couple hours," Dan says. "We'll find a place to get something to eat. There are some more towns down the coast. Also, there's Shëngjin, but I was looking to avoid that place. Bad memories. I was working for Bilo at the time. We were moored in Shëngjin harbor offloading a catch of sea bass. A little girl playing with some friends drowned off the breakwater. I was only a few hundred meters away at the time. I ran to try to help her. I was too late. It was especially difficult for me. You see, I'd lost a daughter a few years earlier. A boating accident."

"I know. When I was researching you," she says, "I found your daughter's obituary in the Quebec papers. Who wrote that?"

"I did."

"That was the most beautiful thing I ever read," she says softly.

Little breaths of breeze slip the flames about. Agata sits on a flat rock by the fire. Dan stands beside her and against the concrete cylinder base of the dome a footstep from the fire. Loops and jagged letters of spray-painted graffiti, a white thespian mask, flare and fade on the wall behind them.

"You were together for a long time, right? Fifteen years?" Agata says.

"Seventeen."

"Impressive. Each of my marriages was three years of cautious lead-up followed by one year of newlywed bliss and one of confused misery followed by several years of desolate sadness," she says. "Cheering myself up. I wish I had a drink."

"Marriage is one solution to the question, but not the only one," Dan offers.

"What question?"

"I don't know what the question is."

Agata leans her elbows on her knees. Her face radiates. Her features dance in the undulating light, her tangled hair.

"Was your wife your first love?"

"Yes, I think so. But I made a mess of everything."

Agata is quiet for a minute. "I think you've done well," she says. "You were a fine husband and partner, from what I can tell. You raised two beautiful and talented daughters. You protected them as well as you could. And you've loved and been loved, powerfully."

She pats his knee with the back of a hand. She says, "I asked the people I found around Madrid who knew you and they directed me to others around Europe, whom I called. You have quite a network of friends out there, you know. I used the pretext that I was looking for someone to help with translation work. I asked if they knew where to find you, that sort of thing. To a person, they lauded you, on every level. I heard a lot of stories about how you strove to help everyone around you in any way you could. You've touched a lot of lives. You've made the world a better place for them. My research didn't lead me to Bilo, but I was absolutely unsurprised to hear him talk about you that way."

Dan circles the little fire and sits beside her on the other side of the flat rock, where there is just room. The fire pops and kicks a little spray of sparks into the dark.

She gazes off at the invisible sea, shakes her head, continues.

172

"But look at us. I'd say of the two of us you're smarter. But I'm tougher. You contain material like a walking library, forging along absorbing things. I, instead, dig like a manic mole, filing information madly. But we were both pretty good at what we did, weren't we? This from the stratospheric vantage point of our mid-late-forties."

"The dust-bins of our lives," Dan says.

"We're a pair, aren't we? How did two smart people like us end up as two down-and-outers like this?"

"If you lose your step, you rattle downward. It's like one of those carnival games where a ball drops into a field of pegs and bounces down, sometimes pausing but always continuing, until it lands in some hole at the bottom. People lay bets on which hole. But once it starts, no one doubts that it will end up at the bottom."

Dan puts his arm around Agata's shoulders and they sit like that for a while, she with her head leaned against him as the fire dies. They rest for a while but soon head out again, the sound of the Ducati's engine lifting the pre-dawn blanket of silence.

CHAPTER 28

ENROUTE TO TIRANA

12 November, Sunday

Smoke-stained curtains hang over the flat landscape and brush up against the mountains inland. Marshes steam. After filling the bike's tank, Dan and Agata eat breakfast in a café along the highway after they cross the Lumi Mat estuary. She pokes at a croissant, tears off a piece and chews for a long time.

"Where are we?"

"Almost to Tirana. Maybe twenty or thirty kilometers. I think we should just get a room and sleep for a while."

She nods. She bites into a segment of orange. "How are you doing on money?"

He shrugs. "OK, I think. Thanks for paying Bilo. He earned it. You're good for karma for the time being." Dan leans back in his seat and considers aloud. "I met some Malians in Madrid. Refugees. They needed money badly. I wish I'd given them more than I did. At the time, I was planning to give everything I collected to Gennie. But my daughter needs love and support, not money, at least not the pittance I can offer."

He has been looking idly over her shoulder at a rack of fly-bitten pastries on the counter. Now he looks back at her.

"I'm sure now. Something inside me has shifted in the past two weeks," he says. "I don't know what or why."

"It's me," she says and half-laughs. "I'm a brilliant influence on everyone I meet." She pulls apart her croissant. Her face is dark-rimmed, depleted, blurred with lack of sleep. "Something inside me is changing also."

She glances over to a group of people at a nearby table. "If I were sitting with that girl, I'd encourage her to fiddle with her hair more. She doesn't look quite stupid enough yet."

Agata drinks her coffee, rattles the cup into the saucer. She says, "I'm sorry, I'm very tired."

They enter an inexpensive hotel along the highway on the outskirts of Tirana among tire shops and blow-dry shops and appliance repair shops. In the arch-ceilinged lobby, tropical fish, platyfish and gourami, and a tilted windmill occupy a glass tank. The floor was once tile, evident from the grid of old grout stains. Electronic Bach minces down from ceiling speakers; odors of cooking onion and cabbage and burning fill the foyer. The room they receive is entirely amber-colored: walls, carpet, blankets, window curtains, bathroom fixtures.

Before lying down, Dan switches on a Greek news channel on a small television mounted on a wall bracket with its tuner box dangling from cables, but he and Agata are both asleep on their respective beds in their clothes before the commercials have ceased and the news begun.

When they wake, it is late afternoon. On the television, a movie rambles. It is Italian, dubbed in Turkish and subtitled in Serbian.

Agata and Dan wash laundry in the bathroom sink using shampoo, rinse, wring and drape it over chairs and a table and doorknobs.

"What day is it?" she asks.

He must think this through. "Sunday, I suspect."

"I'm so hungry I could eat whatever they're having downstairs."

"We'll go out. But you have to put on pants."

She looks down at her white limbs. "We've become domestic together, haven't we? Reminds me, though, I need to shave my legs. I look a little like Janis." She hums a phrase from *Piece of My Heart* as she digs in the pannier for her other jeans. She asks if she can borrow his little Fjallraven knapsack and stuffs the plastic tube into it to bring with her.

Dan parks the motorcycle in a small lot in the center of Tirana, just off the vast oblong of Sheshi Skënderbej with its encirclement of pre-cast concrete and sixties glass. The bike stands in a row of motorcycles and scooters facing a low wall behind Austria Park. The Ducati is large and, even without the panniers, which they left in the hotel room, looms over the rest and takes two spaces.

They find a propitious restaurant and order dinner. They both look around at the little dining room, other diners, the art on the walls. He tells her about sitting behind her in the restaurant in Valencia. She knows, she tells him, and laughs. She relates some of the things she did to lead him along.

"I was unaware how difficult it could be to allow some-one to follow me," she says. "But I came up with a few ideas. Leaving my plane itinerary for you was a stroke of genius, I thought. Also, calling two cabs in Valencia. I knew I had to help you a little. You're an idiot sometimes," she adds gently, placing a hand briefly on top of his where it rests on the table, "but I don't think I've ever trusted anyone as much as I trust you."

Then, when they have re-crossed Austria Park with its low statues and patches of shrubbery, they realize they have turned up the wrong street and must circle back a block to where the

motorcycle is parked. They emerge from shadows between buildings and see a man standing behind the motorcycle.

He is writing on a piece of paper. He appears to be
taking down the license number. He is black-haired and
black-mustached. He does not see them. They stand very still
until he has finished, folded the paper and put it in a pocket and
crossed the street toward some stores and a café opposite.

Dan grabs Agata by the hand and runs to the motorcycle.

"He's watching us," she says.

"I don't care," he says.

He starts the motorcycle and throws on his helmet without
buckling it. She swings on behind him. He rotates the Ducati
and roars through the lot and toward the rear entrance. In the
mirrors, he sees the man coming back into the street to watch
then recede.

Dan swerves through traffic and settles onto the avenue
heading north. In less than ten minutes they have reached the
hotel along the highway. In their room, they stuff their wet
clothing and the rest of their belongings into the panniers.

Back on the bike, they circle the city on the string of
boulevards which convert into the SH3 highway, heading southeast into the dark.

CHAPTER 29

EAST OF TIRANA
12 November, Sunday

On the long straights, Dan accelerates. The Ducati passes through 200 kph and over, slowing only where clots of traffic amass. Wind and roadway howl past. Agata is silent, head turned, holding tightly to Dan's back, her helmet between his shoulder blades, away from the snapping headlights of oncoming cars and trucks. In this manner, they cover fifty kilometers in a matter of minutes.

At the frontier to Macedonia south of Radožka on the lakeshore, the road divides between concrete barriers and legions of arc lights. They pull up to a guard carrying a clipboard and tablet under xenon glare in the weather canopy. His face is square and Slavic, his eyes green. In English, he asks for their passports.

But as they dig in their pockets, he is once and again distracted by a scene unfolding in the opposite lanes, entering Albania. A pair of Albanian guards there have handcuffed three men who stand beside a small van. Flashlights stab into the van's interior.

Looking back to the pair on the motorcycle, the guard points to the panniers. Dan reaches around Agata and pops open the right pannier which contains his belongings. The guard looks down into it, rustles through the wet clothing distastefully. He then slides Agata's passport through a portable scanner. He hands it back to her and runs Dan's through the scanner. A long pause ensues.

"It says your passport has been reported stolen," the guard says to Dan.

"That was me. I thought I'd lost it in Tirana. We went to the embassy, but later that day I found it."

"It says it was reported stolen in Madrid."

The lanes for traffic coming into Albania and going into Macedonia run adjacent, a concrete barrier separating. The clamor of shouting from the arrests has increased. The guard glances repeatedly over their heads at the tumult opposite.

"You know how difficult it is to get them to understand," Dan says. "I called the embassy back that evening to explain that I'd found it. But we needed to leave for Macedonia."

One of the Albanian guards calls to the Macedonian guard. He asks a question. Loud banging rings along the concrete-sided roadways; one of the handcuffed men is kicking the steel side of the van. The man with the flashlight is yelling. From a concrete building roadside, another guard comes at a run with his Kalashnikov in ready position.

The Macedonian guard, distracted and still holding Dan's passport, says, "Wait here." He vaults the concrete barrier toward the unfolding drama.

But Dan does not wait. The guards grapple the three men by the van, who have started to struggle. No one is looking at the people on the lone motorcycle in the eastbound lane. Amidst the yelling and swearing in a multitude of languages and the crackle of radios, Dan clicks the Ducati into gear and glides forward a few lengths, glances into his mirrors, then accelerates slowly into the dark, into opaque and misty Macedonia beyond.

179

CHAPTER 30

OHRID

12 November, Sunday

They circle Struga on the A2 on the northern tip of Lake Ohrid and then slide over to Route 1208 trailing ancient farmland adjacent to the shore. There is no traffic. The surface of the lake shines oily with occasional flakes of color in the moonlight, reflections of distant shore lights stretched and undulating. It is cool, but the black air has taken on the feeling of dry knit silk as it flows over them and touches their skin at wrists and ankles.

At the edge of Ohrid's solemn old center, its cobbled lanes drifted with yellow autumn leaves, they turn into a small hotel not far from the lake. A man in pajamas comes sadly to their ring.

The building is a century and a half old. The ceilings of their room are high and coved, with plaster leaf moldings. Wall paint flakes and peels in spots, revealing decades of never-sufficient revitalization attempts and old color theories. A radiator creaks; the room is hot, but the knob is corroded and will not close. Dan opens a three-meter tall leaded-pane window a hand's width and ties aside the filmy cotton curtain to admit a little air and the occasional night sounds of the old city below. This dissipates some of the elderly shoe smell of the room.

Neither of them sleeps. A digital clock on a table blinks toward midnight. Both of them listen to the sound of slow breathing, neither sure whose breathing it is since the density of the evening, the flight, the fast ride in the dark, lights and police and guns and the inexorable eastward rush has left them both faint. All they know is that they breathe together.

After a while Agata rises from her bed in the near dark, slips off her t-shirt and underpants and comes to his bed where he lies on the sheet spread-eagled. She drapes herself atop him, spilling legs and arms over him, she naked and he in his undershorts. She is taut. Her warmth stretches the length of his. They lie together like this for a minute, her action bringing to the fore the reality of things, and both of them taking a moment to absorb and consider.

Dan brings his palms to Agata's thighs and runs them slowly up her bottom and up her back. She moves her pelvis against him and voices a soft and eternal sound. She rises on outstretched arms and arches her back so her face floats above his. Both faces are molten shadows in the gloom of the old room. She slowly sags toward him, her clavicles bridging together, descending. They kiss. It is an experiment, though arriving late. They kiss again. He rolls her aside, tugging at his shorts, and she waits under him as he kicks them away.

Afterward, she says, "Which side do you prefer to sleep on, left or right?"

"It doesn't matter to me."

"I have a flimsy right shoulder sometimes, so I'll go over here," she says. She wiggles to her left.

"If I had a cigarette, I'd give it to you," he says.

"If I smoked, I'd smoke it," she says.

They lie tightly, their faces, shining lightly in the moonlight, a few centimeters apart. He says, "If we were in some little town along 66 in Nebraska there would be flickering neon outside the window and country music from a bar across the highway. But all we get are church bells reminding us of vespers or compline or whatever it is."

"I thought you knew everything."

"It's Mesonyktikon, the Orthodox midnight office. Corresponds to the prayer in Gethsemane. Preparation for betrayal and all that."

"Of course you knew."

"I didn't want to sound superior," he says, touching her forehead softly with his.

CHAPTER 31

OHRID

13 November, Monday

In the morning, Agata asks, "Do you think we lost him this time?"

"Based on past results, I'd say no," Dan says. "But I don't know how he's finding us. He's keeping his distance, that seems apparent. As if he's watching where we're going but not intercepting us, for some reason. At least not so far."

"What's our next move?"

"I don't know. I have to think it through. They took my passport, so now they think Alvaro is in Macedonia. I guess it's time for me to go back to being faceless Dan, ghost of a man. Let's go for a walk."

They meander past St. Bogorodica Perivlepta and the St. Pantelejmon-Plaosnik monastery. They wander through the market and to the little square with its clock tower and thousand-year-old tree, then to the upper city gate, then to the heavy, towered fortress on the hill and back to the remnant of Greek theater. They eat fish soup and crusty bread in a small restaurant. They speak little, apart from incidentals.

After lunch, they walk back to the hotel, hurrying. They slip into bed again and this time they forge, each knotted and unbound and clasping at whatever gives itself into their hands and arms. It's daylight, so they see and study each other in fine detail. This time, perhaps due to lighting or because the sense each has of being altered, is different. Everything seems clear and definite; no faintness or blur now.

All is urgency and flinging of clothing. Teeth shine. They've both been waiting for this all morning while they were walking around, thinking about it, aching at minimal distance, touching each other with open hands once in a while as they looked at some old frescoes or bits of stonework or vegetables in markets. All morning they kept catching each other looking, wondering, smiling; little anticipatory laughs together under the Roman brickwork, the esplanade of trees along the Boulevard of the Educators.

Her eyes have taken on a different sort of inner illumination, blue verging on green, and direct, as if some uncertainty has been stripped away which held back their light prior. They both grip each other as if they want to ensure themselves of something, or as if they're both already sure of many things.

Her body in his hands is a burning arc of muscle. He is desperate to hold her. His back, his ribs, his arms, to her, are willows and birch. His hands clamber between her legs, and hers return the favor. But there is little need for reassurance or encouragement. She is on top and managing for a while, and then he. Both are fascinated and immediate. Neither wants to laugh, but both occasionally do laugh, though it's not the old smirking laughter of acquiescence that often cushions first embraces. It is laughter like spring greenery.

The centenarian iron bed with its iron springs complains rustily, though certainly this is not its first labors. The radiator continues to clank. From down the hall, a vacuum cleaner in the hands of a housekeeper resounds at its struggle with dry and gritty carpets. The two people in the arch-backed room achieve a moment together when their cries outstrip those of the vacuum cleaner. The machine ceases. Then all is silent in the old hotel.

Later, Dan stands at the window. From the bed, Agata gazes at his naked silhouette against the film of curtain and wan sunlight fingering up to his slender tree-like form from the stony rooftops below, the slack and useful fatigue of his body and its parts, all relaxed forms and curved shadows. He stands beside the frame looking carefully through the slot between the curtain and the wall at the sun leaning broken across the veil of half-leaved trees. In the rising light, he seems to a viewer to float.

They go to dinner, Agata carrying his small knapsack with the tube inside. When they return to the hotel, when they round the corner of the sloping hallway from the top of the stairs, they stop. The door of their room stands open.

Dan slips forward and listens for a minute. There is no sound.

He peeks very slowly around the corner, again waiting for a minute. Finally, he steps into the room.

The two motorcycle panniers lie opened. Their clothing strews underfoot. The mattress dumps askew. The closet door stands ajar.

The desk clerk tells them that a man checked in after them, while they were out having dinner.

"Did he have a black mustache?" Dan asks. The clerk nods.

"Tell me his name."

"I cannot. That's confidential information."

"Tell me or I will call the police. When was your property last inspected?" Dan asks in brittle Macedonian.

The hotelier, a delicate, bald man with small, close-set eyes filled with resistance and little hurts, blinks several times and then says, "He gave the name Nikolai Obli."

"Where is he now?"

"I don't know. He left. He has a black car."

Dan and Agata stand on the porch of the hotel. A slight evening breeze has risen. The lake is shattered quartz.

"We need to leave before he comes back," Dan says. "Then I need to take another look at that tube."

CHAPTER 32

SOUTH OF OHRID
13 November, Monday

They travel only a few kilometers south along the shore of the lake. They pass a low roadside bar in the trees. Along one stone wall stands a row of motorcycles. Dan slows, swings around and comes back to the bar. He parks the Ducati at the far end of the row, in the deep dark under crinkly fall foliage. Across the road, the lake shimmers.

Inside the bar, at the shadowy end of the room, Dan and Agata sit beside each other at a small marble-topped table. A stereo plays Grateful Dead loudly. Five or six other patrons sit at the bar across the room. When *Ripple* comes on, some of them sway dangerously on their barstools, arms draping each other's shoulders, chorusing in deep Slavonic accents.

The old bar sprawls opposite the lakeshore in the moonlight under its proscenium of plane trees. In an adjacent field, Busa shorthorn cows wait behind stone walls along a carved granite water basin. The moon has in fact cleared a swath over western Macedonia, shining like old armor on hills and water, still as slumber now that the wind has died.

Agata hands Dan the plastic tube. He unscrews one of the end caps and inspects it. Then he unscrews the other. He weighs the two in his hands. He sights through the tube and then slips fingers inside and slowly draws out the small painting and lays it in its tissue wrappers on the table.

He looks around the bar. They are alone in their end of the old, limestone-floored, smoke-stained room. Though several men glanced their way, and especially Agata's, when they entered, no one pays attention now.

As he re-inspects the empty tube, Dan muses, "I've been carrying a stolen artwork through the Balkans. People are after us, maybe assassins. I don't know how they're tracking us." An old bronze swan-necked floor-lamp with a cracked sepia shade stands in the corner. Dan swivels it over the painting. The two of them lean further over it.

Dan lifts a corner of the painting, re-settles it. He reaches, hesitates, then touches a fingertip gently to the brushstrokes of the trees, the ivory back of the soft figure in the foreground. The light of the lamp falls like sunshine remembered through filters of greenery and willing laughter. Dan picks up the two endcaps and inspects them, again compares their weights in his hands, holds them up to the light.

He stands and goes to a side table where rests a tray of silverware and takes a butter knife. Seated again, he pokes at one of the endcaps a few times and then jams the tip of the blade into the edge of its lining. He twists and pries and then the cap comes apart. With a small clatter a round object drops onto the wooden floor and rolls under the table. Agata retrieves it.

Dan examines the entrails of a slim device in his palm. He looks at the round object when she hands it back to him.

"That's the battery," he says. "This is the antenna, I think. It was probably set up to come on occasionally and ping the nearest cell tower and then sleep. That way, the battery would last as long as possible."

"So they know we're here?"

Dan shrugs, nods.

The music takes a turn slower. They still sit backs to the room, each holding a glass of McCallan's, looking at nothing. Or perhaps they look at the stones of the wall, their chips and scuffs belying their many-thousand-year meandering in human hands from field to pathway to pasture fence to walls of hovels and barns and eventually the building. Whatever this building has been for the past three centuries, it is now a roadside lakeshore eastern Euro-biker bar, the turmoil of slant-lit stones reflecting great back-waters of time and hardship, or perhaps the faces of the two people who sit quietly with a painting on a table between them.

"You said Henri gave this to you, right?"

Agata nods.

"What haven't you told me about Henri?"

She sits quietly for a minute, sips more whiskey. "He's with Interpol. He's undercover."

Eventually, Dan says, "So you didn't find that this rose to the level of something to tell me about."

She speaks through her fingers which cover her mouth. "I didn't want to involve you."

They sit with their backs to the room, alone together. The little table faces the wall. Shadows lie long along the stones of the wall and under the hewn beams, under the smoke-tarnished ceiling. The small cacophony swells and diminishes periodically behind them somewhere toward the other end of the space where the bar humbly gestures toward glitter and warmth, its row of souls leaning into the evening with their backs to Dan and Agata.

"What a fool I am. I needed someone to help. Someone to protect. Maybe even someone to love. So tired of being cold and alone. Mostly tired of being no use to anyone. An extran-

189

eous spirit. And then there you stood in your beret and your boots, with your frightened eyes." He says this not to Agata but to the table.

"You were trying to protect me. And I was trying to protect you. I thought if we could just get loose of the people tracking us we could get this cleared up. Erase the problem for everyone."

Dan says, "You still haven't explained what you're planning to do with it. If I'm carrying you and the painting somewhere, it would be fair for me to know where and why, don't you think?"

"Henri said to hold onto it. He didn't have time to deliver it to the right people. He was still trying to get more information. He trusted me. He said to just keep it safe for a few days, and then he would meet me or send me further directions somehow. He said to move south, toward Greece, if I could. I was so relieved when you said that's the direction you were going and had found a way to get there under the radar."

Agata reaches to the painting and touches it lightly with a fingertip. "The handover has to be choreographed," she says. "You can't just walk into a local police station with a priceless stolen artwork. It may well just disappear again, and who knows what will happen to you. But Henri hasn't contacted me. I checked again before we went to dinner."

Dan lays the tissue paper back over the painting and rolls it slowly just narrow enough to fit into the tube. He slips the tube uncapped back into the knapsack.

"I hope I was useful to you."

"Please," she says. "Please don't."

The music now rollicks again. Singing has picked up. Another chorus escalates.

"They're not far behind. If that thing sent a signal, they'll be here soon." Dan stands and takes the knife back to the silverware table and drops the whole endcap and the shattered one into a small trash can underneath.

Outside, on the slope to the lake, he zips his coat and slides on his helmet in the sheer moonlight. His eyes shine with it until he snaps down the visor, blanking his face. Agata stands beside him holding the knapsack with the tube inside.

"Where are you going?" she asks. "How are you going to get anywhere with no passport?"

He says nothing as he inserts the key and starts the motorcycle, clicks the shifter to neutral and lets out the clutch. He sits on it, one hand resting on the softly vibrating tank as the engine warms. He looks out over the silken lake, then at her, still faceless.

"I don't know."

Her expression is a wall of compassion and fear. "You're stuck in Macedonia. You have no identity again."

He lifts the visor of his helmet. He looks at her with a countenance of gratitude for stating the obvious.

He says, "Where are you going?"

"I need to get to Greece," she says. "I don't know how."

His eyes reflect hers. They glitter with the light off the water, the light of distance and judgment and experience and folly.

"Please," she says standing with the knapsack tight in both hands and her back to the silver lake.

"The problem with you," he says, his hands resting on his thighs, "isn't that you lie about things. It's that you never tell the whole story."

"Please," she says again.

"Which is essentially the same."

"I don't know the whole story. I'm making it up as I go along. Isn't that how you've survived?"

Dan looks down at the motorcycle's glowing gauges, then up to the row of trees along the silver stone wall and the silver cows standing stock still just beyond, watching.

He rolls the bike slowly forward off its stand, settles, clicks it into gear, sits there for another full minute. "Get on," he says.

CHAPTER 33

MACEDONIAN BORDER

13 November, Monday

Route 501 traces the shore of Lake Ohrid southward through Lagadin and Elshani, sometimes atop segments of ancient retaining wall with the water dozing at its toes. They pass solemn stands of apartments, shuttered campgrounds and slat-sided vacation houses; the ground steps onto a dry plateau, clotted with the low evergreens called molika.

A knee-high lynx crosses in the motorcycle's headlight, and a kilometer further a fox pauses wayside, saucer-eyed and blade-eared. Night air sweeps watery cool past the riders. Bats stitch and flicker the sky along the thicker-wooded stretches.

In this landscape barely sketched in the light of an old quarter moon, they come to a fork in the road, but Dan knows which way to go, and Agata leans into the turn with him.

The rising road shrugs off the forests. A shoulder of the massif soars to the north. The ground is limestone with low sedge in its seams. To the southwest, the valley falls away to polished lake and a satin hip of distant Albania recumbent in the moonlight.

At the pass, for a brief rest, Dan pulls off in a graveled area by a grouping of signs and shelters. The two of them gaze out over the naked landscape. Now nearly two weeks into their journey, the moon's pocked blue surface is as sharp as the terrestrial tableau below. Velvet valleys shuffle off. The mirror of the lake and the aged solemnity of supine rock ridges frame the view.

Agata tips up the visor of her helmet and breathes in the stony night air, much cooler here than along the placid shoreline. Neither speaks. The pause on their flight is tribute to being and brevity.

Beyond the pass, the road descends on a long wavering note and then vanishes into the pines again, sweeping and dancing. The tone of the motorcycle's engine rises and falls. Its inertia drapes over them right and left, flickering. Warm between and beneath them, the machine hums. They ride close and wrapped, two beings locked under cold sky.

Along Lake Prespa, the road aims restlessly southward again and diminishes in quality, eventually devolving into a dirt track at the point that a blocky old border station appears, although this crossing has been decommissioned and fenced with coiled razor wire.

The marshy lakeshore lies a hundred meters to the west. But on the left, dry hills ascend, dotted in clefts with scrubby pines and willows. All is pale and visible, especially after Dan fiddles with the motorcycle's switches and turns off the headlight. They sit in the ambient light for another minute, eyes adjusting, the low rumble of the bike's idling engine the only sound in the night.

"Hold on," Dan says.

He swivels the bike slowly and heads to the east, uphill, on a herder's trail, maneuvering slowly among rocks and occasional dung piles. The motorcycle bounces and sways under them. Agata braces herself between the pillion handle and Dan, knees tight, the little knapsack with its cargo bouncing on her back.

They proceed by moonlight alone. The trail ascends, evidently aiming slowly toward higher hills, scabby pastures. The path steepens. The rear tire skids a few times. Rocks click and scuffle into the grass.

They cross a gentle, bare ridge. On the far side, back in the trees, Dan snakes the motorcycle through a maze of thickets and over the polished stones of a dry creek bed, guns it slightly as they come up the rise beyond, kneeing through dried underbrush. A smooth grassy area ensues and then a fence. The fence merges into a low stone wall. He turns the bike through a gap in the wall and onto a two track. The track angles uphill and then sharply south past a collection of small, dark-windowed farm buildings behind another stone wall and then over a plank wooden bridge. They turn onto an unpaved but improved road.

"Where are we?" Agata asks.

"Greece," Dan says.

CHAPTER 34

KASTRAKI

14 November, Tuesday

Sunrise approaches. The way south widens into a farm road which laces the edges of latent bean and pepper fields packed along the shores of Lake Prespa and a low rise of dessicated hills to the north. As they emerge slowly from shadowed foothills, Dan glances constantly at the mirrors. The road improves and is empty of traffic.

In Kastoria, on its little thumb on the shore of Lake Orestiada, they fill the gas tank at a Shell station. They buy pastries and oranges and stiff coffees in paper cups from a café adjacent. They spread a map over a picnic table beside the building in the placid, sketchy sunlight and trace a projected path down the tail of the Dinarics behind and ahead.

They ride on along a desolate, striking valley. The snowy dinosaur-spine of Mount Olympus hovers far across Thessaly. Ice floes of low clouds disperse. The day gradually warms. Agata begins to slump against Dan's back. On a couple of occasions, she slips a little and then grips again.

They cross an arm of the Pindus, parched and pungent air redolent of drying garrigue. Scents of oleander, bay, and juniper rise. Cirrus smears the sky. The valley below, blurred forest

196

of evergreen oak, dogwood, fir and sycamore, lounges in dusty autumn haze. Dan knows this area well.

Down the river valley lies Kalabaka with its clatter and signs and barking traffic. They sweep through a roundabout and motor up into Kastraki and turn on a side road down into a ravine.

Scattered half-plastered buildings angle toward old, scruffy orchards dotted with wandering chickens. On the uphill side, below bulbous reddish-grey cliffs, they pull into the drive of a tidy iron-gated guesthouse.

A woman comes to the knock at the door of the guesthouse. She is dark-haired and tall. She wears a greyish-green cardigan and jeans, sneakers and a thin string of pearls, though it is only mid-morning. She holds a little boy by the hand. Across the threshold, she gazes at Dan for a moment, drops the boy's hand and says, "Dan." She embraces him.

In the main room, a fireplace in sleek Aegean stucco, white as snow, rises under twenty-foot timbered ceilings. The building is clean and sharp, its pale pine trim highly varnished.

"We're passing through, Ellie. We've been traveling all night. Do you have a room?"

She does indeed have a room. In fact, all five guestrooms are vacant owing to the off-season and the Greek economy.

"Sleep all day," she says.

The sheets are cool. Morning rolls to noon outside the open window but all is quiet save for an occasional clunk and singsong voicing from the boy's play downstairs and sporadic gabble from chickens down the hill in the ravine. They do sleep all day.

Late afternoon, at Agata's suggestion, she and Dan visit a salon in Kastraki recommended by Ellie. They both have their hair shampooed and trimmed. Agata's shade has faded over the

197

past few weeks. Her hair is now pale reddish-blonde, slightly streaked, blonde-rooted, a grey strand here and there. The stylist admires her and says, "Beautiful, beautiful."

Dan turns in his chair under his black plastic cape and smiles at her.

After dark they walk up the road with Ellie, her husband Kostas and the boy, Giorgio, who dances and races ahead, shouting in the citrus and juniper evening.

They eat at a long, rough table in a smoke-black-timbered old barn of a restaurant belonging to Kostas' mother. The restaurant fills slowly with early-evening local crowd. A man in a Nike jacket plays a tzouras with another man, in a plaid shirt and neckerchief, playing guitar. Shouting music, spontaneous ballads ring through the noisy crowd. In a high stone fireplace at one end of the room, whole lambs and a pig roast and sizzle over beechwood coals.

Ellie and Kostas introduce Dan and Agata to an endless stream of hand-shaking, back-clapping people, many of whom remember Dan from his stints here tutoring teenage students in English and French in the mornings and driving farm tractors among the ancient, hoary olives in the afternoons.

Kostas' mother, sturdy and stiff in apron and cap, directs several dark-eyed boys and girls who deliver platters to tables with mountains of sausages and roasted lamb, peppers stuffed with feta, eggplant stuffed with onions, garlic and herbs. More platters arrive bearing dolmades, stuffed zucchini, stuffed tomatoes, green salads and red salads and grainy salads with mint.

The two couples open a bottle of retsina and it is quickly emptied, so they open another, and before long, another. Their table bears resemblance to the wreckage of a medieval banquet. Giorgio plays, sings, cavorts, tugging sleeves and hands. "Only child," Ellie apologizes.

198

A lull in the music and singing softens the room for a few minutes and makes conversation more plausible.

"Ellie," Dan says to Agata, "has a doctorate in political science. Kostas is a restorer of ancient sculpture. But they decided to come back to run the family guesthouse."

"Someday we will get back to our chosen professions," Kostas says. "Maybe. When the world we have inherited permits us."

"For now, this is a good life," Ellie says, combing her hair back with her fingers, but her voice and expression darken. "We meet a lot of people. Guests who venture here to visit the monasteries. We're a long way from the islands. People who come here tend to be those who love Greece, not just the fun-times image of Greece. The visitors who pass through our household are a good introduction to the wider world for Giorgio. Kostas and I argue about it sometimes. I don't want Giorgio to grow up in a place that's, what is the word?"

"Provincial," Dan says.

"Yes, provincial. But Kostas wants Giorgio to have the safe and comfortable small-town origin that he had. I agree with Kostas about that. But sometimes it's hard being here. Feeling eternally locked down, just trying to make ends meet. It can be a sort of prison. A pleasant prison."

Ellie shrugs and looks up from her plate at Agata. "Each of us alone and all clinging together in our world of aging grace and immutable change," Ellie says.

"Things will transform," Kostas says. "They must. Or it's the end of Greece. The end of history."

When Ellie and Kostas are away from the table, Dan says to Agata, "I know you are anxious to get wherever you're going. But I'm exhausted. I need a little time to think and understand, figure out more of what's going on and my next steps. I'm staying here tomorrow. We can go for a walk. See the monasteries. Or if you prefer, you can catch a bus from here to wherever you need to go. I can take you to the station in Kalabaka first thing."

"I'm staying with you," Agata says. "A while longer. If that's okay with you."

CHAPTER 35

METEORA
15 November, Wednesday

In the morning, dense mist clogs the valley, but the sky shifts from silver to blues as, on the motorcycle, luggage left in the guesthouse, and following a good night's rest, Dan and Agata ascend narrow switchbacks toward the plateau. They park the bike in a wide space along the road and climb shaded and damp stone steps to Roussanou soaring on its pillar of rock. Chilly green air seeps downward through the trees. From the circular platform just below the entrance they view out over the sea of fog in the valley.

They visit Great Meteoron. Low singing emerges as they ascend the long stairwells carved into the cliffside, and the singing illuminates the shadows under the cornices of rock.

Dan and Agata drift through the sepulchral church, squinting up at frescoes of the Last Judgment and the Punishment of the Damned. They run their hands over the curves of the spindle that hoists baskets and netted pallets from the valley below, and they wander a wine cellar between rows of ancient, seedy casks evocative of winnowed existence and dry-rot. All is the architecture of accretion, built of hand-wrought stone and long-ago painted stone and stone buttressed with fraying timbers, the mountain's constitution and its hue and temperature.

They visit Varlaam clustered on the next pillar down the ridge. They ascend meticulously swept steps and courtyards, briefly view more frescoes. From the rectory floats the scent of fresh-baked barley bread, toasting and buttered.

Later, away from the road and other wanderers, they sit on a flat plate of rock on the clifftop back from the moss-slick curve over the precipice. It is so quiet they hear wind through the wing feathers of peregrine riding updrafts along the cliffs. Past visitors seated on this rock carved initials into the soft sandstone. The letters have worn smooth.

Their heels slip on lichen and tiny pebbles and snail shells. Mist in the valley has mostly cleared but for scraps in the trees along the river. A blur hangs over Kalabaka, but the air higher and across the valley and over the plateau behind them is watery clear.

"That's the Monastery of the Holy Trinity, Agia Triada, over there," Dan says, pointing to another lean stone structure hunched on a pinnacle a kilometer south. "The one where they filmed a James Bond movie."

"I seem to remember this view," Agata says. "Maybe I saw that movie."

These statements are among the first they have exchanged this quiet morning. They sit close together, but slanted. There is nothing to do for a few minutes but observe the canted wedges and pancaked pillars of sandstone dense with conglomerate ringing the steep-floored valley, long silver and charcoal gowns of water stains descending cliffs to the valley floor.

"*The feeling of being lost in time and geography with months and years hazily sparkling ahead in a prospect of inconjecturable magic,*" Dan says.

Agata turns to look at him.

"That's from Patrick Leigh Fermor, my favorite writer of Europe-wandering. I quote it here for the irony."

She nods, sits quietly for a minute.

"Why are you still with me?" she says. "If I were you I would have left me behind way back in Dubrovnik."

Dan gives this due consideration before replying.

"We need each other. We've gotten this far – it could be that we're good together. Why didn't you just fly out of Dubrovnik to wherever you're going?"

"Because you weren't leaving that way. You were going by motorcycle."

They remain seated this way for several minutes, close, hips touching but torsos angled apart, elbows on knees, facing slightly outward from each other, a composition of attitude or perhaps just the curvature of the rock. Dan picks up a pebble and flicks it and it clicks off the decline and disappears over the side into suspended silence.

"It was sad what Kostas was saying," Agata says. "About the end of Greece."

Dan nods agreement. "Kostas has thought about it a lot. We had many late-night conversations. He sees it from his vantage point, from the eyes of the ancient sculptures he worked on, buried for thousands of years and then brought back into new solitude and destruction. Some sort of metaphor there. Wisdom and hopelessness. Shelley's shattered visage frowning up from the sands of time."

"Or Fukuyama's last man staring sadly forward into the wreckage of liberal democracy."

Dan nods again. "You see what I mean about us being good together."

203

A twiggy, stooped man comes along the scant trail over the crest. He is dark-capped and wears a khaki canvas vest. He carries binoculars and a guide to birds of Thessaly. He nods to Dan and Agata and passes behind them heading toward the scarp where the mud of swallows' nests washes gradually into the valley.

"What fascinates me," Agata says, "is how these monks dedicated themselves so completely to their little communities. The labor of building these places, stone by stone, going up and down the cliffs with ropes and handmade ladders, praying together, breaking bread together. The sweat, the silence, the cold mountain rain, the misery, and always the fear of the outside world, the Ottomans. Such small groups, too."

"Between them, a matter of trust," Dan says.

"Trust," Agata says. "My father was the only person I ever trusted. He was unapproachable, of course, like most of the men I adore. Silent and chilled, like the piles of money he built, brick by gold brick. But he contained me. He held me on his lap when I was small and looked into my eyes, he held me by the shoulders when I was a teenager and looked into my eyes, he held me by the hands when I got married and looked into my eyes."

They sit silent for a minute. Clouds of swallows settle on distant branches and set to squalling, then fall quiet.

"Maybe he never had much to say, just some eye-looking," she continues. "He was just always there in the distance, but calming, like eternity. Until he died very suddenly the summer before I wrote the article at the *Times*. Unexpectedly. The same way eternity died. Left me bereft. No one else has ever drawn my trust. I've been alone. Until you came along, Daniel. With your bookishness and your faith in some humanistic ideal you can't put your finger on and your damnable reliability. You make me feel like everything is going to be okay. It's very unfair of you."

"My bad upbringing," he says.

"I feel better when I'm around you, but when I step back, I realize I have no reason to feel anything other than what I always feel: frightened and solitary."

"The modern condition."

Another couple ambles by along the crest of the cliff, handsome young people chatting lowly in Spanish. They stop not far from Dan and Agata and take a photo of the monastery across the gorge with a phone on a stick, then move slowly on.

A few minutes pass in silence after the couple has passed. Then Agata says just above a whisper, "I know where the rest of the paintings are."

Dan does not respond to this. "Athens," she says.

Still Dan is silent, so she clears her throat and continues.

"Alvaro has a house there. It's in Anafiotika up along the base of the Acropolis. That's a settlement of Greek refugees from Smyrna. Alvaro is Greek, but his family lived in Turkey until the genocide began. I think his grandparents came to Athens about 1915. It's a family house, not actually Alvaro's, but he goes there sometimes. His mother still lives there. He took me there once," Agata relates without looking at him. She speaks softly into the bluish void in front of them.

"I know I said I hadn't met him in person," she says. "That wasn't quite true. It was never something I wanted. But I went with him on a couple of trips. A few trips. Once to Athens. He showed me the paintings when we were there. He had all four of them stored in an old trunk in his house. Just sitting there with his mother pottering about with her brooms and geraniums. The Modigliani, the Picasso, the Braque, the Léger. They had been dispersed, but he acquired them various ways. Brought them back together. He didn't tell me how and I didn't ask."

She pauses for a while, letting things settle in for both of them. "He told me I was the only one who knew," she continues. "He said he hadn't shown them to anyone else. At that time, he was only missing the Matisse. It was true what I said about him wanting me to come to South America with him. He said he would bring the paintings and we would sell them in Recife or Mar del Plata. Underground. He knows people everywhere. I think he was in love with me, or he thought he was. It's so weird and terrible because the two of you look so similar, but he's monstrous. He loved me and I loathed him. I love you and you probably loathe me."

After another pause, she says, "And it's true what I said about refusing to go with him when he asked me. All of that is true. I'm running from him now. He wants me dead. I know it."

The two of them sit resting from this for a minute. Agata's breathing slowly calms. Dan rubs his forehead with a palm and squints as if attempting to erase a headache.

Eventually he says, "Love and death. Aren't we a little too old to be using silly words like that?"

"You use them," she says softly. "You just don't say them out loud."

Dan sits gazing down at the rock for a while and then says, "I asked once before: What are you doing with the Matisse?"

"The part I told you about it was true, too. Mostly. Henri was drafted by Alvaro to do some work for him, but it wasn't because of blackmail. Henri had inserted himself into Alvaro's group. He really is an undercover agent. They were pretty sure Alvaro had some of the paintings, but they didn't know where. They knew he was trying to get the Matisse. So they made a copy, a forgery. They set it up somewhere it wouldn't be difficult to steal, in a house in the hills above Antibes. They were trying to lure him."

She brushes at an ant which has crawled onto her leg. She reaches down and pulls up a sock. She continues, "Then Henri went to Alvaro and told him he knew where the Matisse was. This was intended to induce Alvaro to tell him about the rest of the paintings. I didn't know what they were up to. But I later told Henri that I had seen the Matisse. Then our trip started, and the next thing I knew Henri was handing the painting to me in Rome."

Dan says, "So you knew where the other paintings were all along."

"Yes."

"But you didn't tell Henri."

"No."

"And now Henri is probably dead."

"I don't know. I hope not. Henri is pretty good at taking care of himself. He has the whole French police system behind him."

Dan asks, "Why didn't you tell Henri about the other paintings?"

"Protecting the hand I was dealt."

"Why are you holding onto the Matisse?"

"Strengthening the hand I was dealt."

Dan turns to look at Agata directly.

"Why are you taking it to Athens? Tell me the truth this time. All of it."

"I'm going to march into Interpol with all five paintings. I'll tell them the story. It will be my redemption. It will cause a worldwide sensation, you realize. I'll write a book. Maybe then I will go home to America. Put the past behind me."

Down the ridge some distance, a flock of swallows rises. They swirl and dart, crying.

She continues, "It's how godless people like us find redemption, you know. Little acts of beauty and contrition. Acts of charity. Acts of sacrifice. Acts of absolution."

A truck labors on the ascent in the gorge. A pair of children race by behind them, laughing.

"How do you know Alvaro hasn't already collected the other paintings from Athens after he learned the Matisse had been taken?" Dan says.

"He wouldn't send someone else for that. He'd do it himself. He just reported his passport stolen to try to stop you from getting anywhere. It will take a little time before he has a replacement. He can't leave the continent without one."

All remains quiet around them. Nothing much has changed about the morning except that while they have been sitting on the rock the sun has grown faintly warmer and the mist has finally dissolved from the trees along the distant river.

"Agata, you said Alvaro knows your secret, the whole business with the article you wrote. If you break him, he'll expose you."

"I'll say he made it up. He will be at the center of the story I'm telling. He will be in prison, he and his friends. I can prove it all. I can dig up the rest of the story, the parts I don't know yet. Who will believe him, a thief and murderer, over me, a righter of wrongs?"

Dan sits apparently evaluating all that Agata has said for several minutes, and she remains silent for him to do this. He sighs once. His eyes track the path of a hawk high against the cliffs across the valley until it disappears over the ridge. He looks back at Agata.

"Tell me something. Honestly. Are you going to just take the other paintings and sell them yourself?"

She shakes her head and ticks off on her fingers. "One, I wouldn't know how, probably get myself killed. Two, if I was going to do that I wouldn't have told you about them. Three, I'm trying to get back to the world of the living, not burrow deeper into obscurity and solitude and perpetual hiding and flight.

"On the other hand," she continues, eyes dropping and then coming back up to his, "if you wanted to take them with me, that would be different. It crossed my mind. The paintings are already ghosts, after all, like we are. We could just hang them in our living room in Quebec or Greenwich and tell friends at our dinner parties that they were prints. Enjoy them all our lives. Our secret forever. Then in our wills return them to the museum so there's a happy ending for everyone."

"Happy endings," Dan says. "Plenty of those where I come from."

"Cynic."

"Romantic."

"Come on, Dan, you know you're intrigued."

"Dreamer."

"Idealist," she says.

"Optimist."

"Perfectionist."

"I guess we've gotten to know each other," Dan says.

"You're not angry with me?"

"What would we gain from anger?" he says.

Late that afternoon, in the guesthouse, Dan dries dishes and talks with Ellie in the kitchen. Agata checks her email on Ellie's laptop in the living room.

"Dan," Agata calls. He stops, looks across at her, an expression of recognition on his face, the tone of her voice.

He reads over her shoulder. The email states: *Henri is dead.*

We're coming for you. Tell your friend Dan we have his daughter. This one, unlike the last, has a sender address. It is Tranchard's.

Dan borrows Ellie's phone, dials Angelique's number in Paris.

"Hello?"

"Angelique, it's Dan." He says this as he steps onto the porch and closes the door behind. "Where's Gennie? Have you seen her?"

"She's sitting here beside me. We're in the kitchen. What's going on? Where are you?"

"Is anyone else there?"

"Just Gregor. He's upstairs."

"Lock the doors and windows and don't go anywhere. It's critical. Call the police and tell them someone may be stalking Gennie. I'll send you a photo that you can give them."

"Dan, you're scaring me. What is going on?"

"Better yet. Does your boyfriend, the count, have a fast car?"

"I don't know if it's fast. A big Mercedes."

"You said he has a place up near Gstaad, right?"

"Yes."

"And it's a safe place?"

"It's a little fortress. And he has staff there. A security system. Dogs."

"Have him drive you and Gennie up there. Tonight. Get there as soon as possible. When you get there, call the police in Bern and give them the photo, too. It's a photo I took of two men in Madrid. They may be looking for Gennie."

"What have you gotten into? Dan, for God's sake."

"I'll explain everything," he says. "I promise."

"Have you done something reckless again?"

"I promise."

Angelique's voice peaks. "Have you done something to put Gennie in danger?"

"Angie, I promise."

"I can't believe this is happening. I feel sick."

"If Gennie wants her boyfriend to go along, that's fine. Make a little holiday of it. But don't take much time. Just get out of Paris quickly and quietly. Tonight. Please. Do this for me."

When Dan comes back from the porch, Agata is talking to Ellie in the kitchen. "Some business partners that we need to deal with," he hears Agata saying.

Dan takes Agata into the living room where they whisper by the tall fireplace.

"I talked to Angelique. Gennie is fine. They were lying. I think they're bluffing. I don't think they know where we are. Tell me the address of the house in Athens so I can find it on the map, get oriented."

Agata opens her mail on the laptop again and finds the address. Then she hurries to the bedroom. Dan stays at the computer for a while.

In the bedroom, Agata folds and packs her clothing in the pannier and stuffs in the tube. She straightens and looks at him when he comes in.

He says, "We've driven too many nights. Nothing we can do there right now. We'll sleep here a few hours. We'll be in Athens in the morning. We'll find the place and take a look."

They lie together in the bed unclothed in the cool of the evening for a while in the dark. Then Dan gets up and switches on a small light. He takes the tube from the pannier and the painting from the tube. He spreads it carefully on the bed and removes the tissue paper. Agata stands beside him. They are very close, touching, a bridge of warmth, nude forms in the room looking at nude forms in the painting, both just studying, the lift of brighter colors in the middle, the shades of velvety green and turquoise, the strong, even composition and sure hand.

Dan sets the painting aside. They straighten together by the bed. Dan takes Agata's hand in one hand and then her waist in his other. He slowly wraps his arms around her, and she around him. Her face is against his chest. They stand tightly together for a minute. His palms descend her back, her waist.

They sink to the bed and wrap together with the ferocity of hope and the desperation of finality.

CHAPTER 36

THE ROAD TO DELPHI

16 November, Thursday

They are up before sunrise. In the dark outside the house, Dan slides on his helmet and zips his coat tightly. "We need to hurry," he says, "but I'm concerned about the Greek police. Illegitimate Croatian license plate, no driver's license, no passport. They sometimes set up checkpoints. I think instead of going on the freeway down the coast, we'll take the western route around the mountains. It's about the same distance."

They descend from the dry, humped ranges into the grey-green valley along the river. The road winds endlessly through billowing cloaks of wild thicket and fruit orchards embedded in slight pastures along the stony riverbed.

South of Trikala, the highway flattens and straightens as hills dissipate behind. Soon, more mountains rise ahead. Sunrise opens the view, first a washed grey and then corrugated shades of lime and lavender. Windows of distant houses cast gold across scented fields: sugar beets, wheat, peach, nectarine and apple orchards, and always everywhere olives.

Dan pushes the speed limit and sweeps past cars and trucks. The big bike carries its passengers effortlessly a hundred kilometers in an hour, despite the road snaking small towns and roundabouts.

They cross the broad coastal plain, once shallow sea, where lie the bones of Athenian and Spartan soldiers, past the end of the Malian Gulf off the Aegean, departing southwest again just before Thermopylae.

As the morning expands and they travel south, the air rapidly warms. Agata unzips her lambskin coat, then eventually slips it off, opens the pannier to her right and stuffs it in, her knees squeezing Dan tightly, all at speed on a curving road. She rides now in her turtleneck shirtsleeves, holding firmly to him again.

For a while, she rides with her visor up. Big sunglasses mirror the sky, equal shadows beneath. Her head rests against Dan's back, solemn face turned aside, eastward, to the ululations of wind and motor. Her arms wrap him. His posture is brave against her grip on the old lonesome route.

Ancient stony landscapes, fiery shattered mountains, drift by in the reflections in her glasses. The great northern arc of the Mediterranean has passed behind them, its naked terrain, skeletons of mountains and time, the endless sweep of human migration against geologic eternities, all in the space of a breath, a single slow sigh of the dying season.

On the east, Mount Parnassus rises magnetic behind the ridges. In the distance ahead through the cupped hands of the valley shine fragments of the Sea of Corinth. They switchback easterly up into the sleep-eyed town of Delphi and stop just beyond, high on the breast of the valley.

"We need a short rest," Dan says.

They park along the road, stretch and walk to the embankment to look out over the gorge. They turn together and look up the steep hill to the travertine ruins shining above through the trees.

214

"I would like to see it," says Agata.

So they hike up the Via Sacra as it bends among the treasuries and to the Temple of Apollo. Crested larks and dark-throated thrushes whistle and call, and a northern goshawk shrieks solitary once somewhere over the ridge. Morning cicadas hum. The sunbaked theater ascends the hillside above. It is still early, and tourists are scant.

"That's the Omphalos," Dan says, pointing to a stone base in the center of a platform. "The oracle. Site of the prophesy. The navel of the world."

"I want to ask a question and see what she says."

"Go ahead."

Agata closes her eyes and stands still for a full minute, her face slightly upturned in the brilliant sunshine, her feet on moss-laced, cracked and timeworn rocks.

From where he stands a few paces away, Dan says, "Did she answer?" His voice is a whisper, but bell-clear among the quiet stones.

"Of course."

Dan nods. "Funny thing about the future," he says. "One spends a lot of time asking what will happen to me, my loved ones, how much time do I have, what should I do? But we already know the answers. That was the oracle's secret, I've always thought."

"My point precisely," Agata says.

They move together to stand for several more minutes in silence. Dan reaches over and takes Agata's hand.

"I'm sorry, Dan," she says. "About everything."

"So am I, Agata," he says.

On their descent from the Omphalos, a woman sits near the vacant pathway among the ribcages of the treasuries. As they pass her, Dan stops. He looks at the woman. She is dark-skinned and dressed in stitched, colorful and shapeless clothing. Her desiccated little body vanishes within layered skirts. Beside her on the ancient stones rests a cloth shopping bag emblazoned with printed flowers. Its contents bulge the bag's coarse fabric. Agata stops a step further and turns to look back at Dan, and then at the woman.

The face of the woman remains cool, rigid, but her black eyes blaze back the sun at Dan. Slowly, she lifts a palm skyward. Her wrists knot with veins and tendons, scarred skin. She is a doppelganger of the woman Dan saw when he exited Iglesia de las Trinitarias Descalzas in Madrid two weeks earlier. She looks up at him in the same manner as that other ageless person. She holds out her quiet hand in the same gesture. But millions of itinerant, mendicant refugees salt Europe.

"Do I know you?" Dan asks in Greek. He steps toward the woman. She watches him take his step. She watches him stop and stand before her.

"What did you come here to ask?" she says finally. Her cloudy, clotted voice springs from the rocks, some variant of old Romanian, a voice Dan understands. Above, Delphi hums its songs. Still, the birds in the trees ring. Some human calls, streaked brush-strokes of voices, meander up the hillside through the ruins.

Dan considers this. "I came to ask what it is that I'm following," he says in her language.

The woman, seated on a pad of stone chiseled millennia ago, nods. She reaches down and touches one of her legs, caresses a spot on a calf as if it is sore. Then with a wrist she wipes her dry nose. She gradually rolls her eyes up to Dan.

"You are not a follower," she says. "If you were, you would not have made it this far."

The three people stand in the sun for a full minute. Then Dan offers the woman some money, a few of the remaining bills in his wallet. She does not decline. She grips the bills and stuffs them into her cloth bag and wipes her nose again.

East of Delphi, the road winds through mountain resort towns with dormant ski lifts spiking the far ridges. Then it begins its long, slow descent to its origin. The silent pair ride through the shift from olives to orange groves like an ancient story unfolding into the modern clamor of Athens.

CHAPTER 37

ATHENS
16 November, Thursday

Dan and Agata ride the broad-shouldered motorcycle into the streets of the city. They cruise Dirrachiou on a diagonal and then Domokou due south past the train station and the central market and then toward Syntagma Square.

Traffic grows increasingly dense. Dan amplifies Greek driving habits, slewing the bike between cars and alongside trucks, carving out passing lanes where no lanes exist, crowding crosswalks. A troop of school children in matching plaid out-fits crosses the street, their teachers holding up hands to stop oncoming cars. A man on a bicycle loaded with sacks of onions veers across three lanes. A few onions slip from holes in netting and bounce along the pavement.

Gaggles of scooters and motorbikes, commuters racing to work, cluster at each stoplight, revving. Dan threads up among them, the low throat of the Ducati turning heads, eyes surveying the two riders in black jackets and matching black full-faced helmets.

They work this way through Athens, gleaming in morning sunshine, cradled in its grand circle of hills spilling slowly down to its metal and stone-dust harbor. Central, the low dry-forested con-clusion of the Acropolis rests under its shining Parthenon crown.

At the lower end of Syntagma, Dan skims through little tributaries of pedestrians and maneuvers along side streets southward. Customers already cluster the booths of food and drink street vendors. Everywhere the scents of charcoal and roasting meat float.

Dan knows this city, but so does Agata. "Go that way," she says, pointing. "Take this street."

They approach as close as they can the steep lanes of Plaka Anafiotika on the motorcycle and then park on a sloping cobbled alley in the black shade of a white building. Along an adjacent wall, a line of wind chimes lights the morning with gentle brass and glass. Agata takes the knapsack with the plastic tube from the pannier. She leads.

They ascend lower walkways past cafés where proprietors are just setting out tables and chairs for the day. Shops selling porcelain bowls, stone walls hung with dresses in filmy fabrics on wooden hangers, and art studios line the narrow streets. Deep green foliage overhangs corners; flowers in pots dangle from eaves.

Agata and Dan zigzag up steps of mortar and marble fragments and branch into the residential neighborhood higher on the hillside. Low creamy, chocolate, sky-blue-trimmed stone houses surround them.

Agata comes to a corner and stops. The two of them stand still, breathing from the climb. They are damp.

She points to a doorway ahead and a little to the right in a corner before the point at which the path turns and makes its final ascent to an Acropolis access road.

All is quiet. A colorful cat passes, heading downhill in the deep shade of the wall out of the reflected whiteness. It turns to look at them. Somewhere, a baby cries. A radio blares in a house. Distant hammering and sawing echoes. Leaves ripple in the heat.

219

"Are you sure?" he says.

She nods. "What are you going to say?" she whispers.

"I'll make something up."

He climbs the pair of stone steps before the door. She stays behind ten meters on the pathway. He stands listening.

Then he knocks softly on the door panel. He listens. He knocks again, louder.

Agata advances slowly until she is at the base of the steps to the house.

A window cuts through the thick, whitewashed stone wall an arm's length to the left of the door. Blue and yellow flowers drape from a wooden box on its sill. Dan steps left and leans to look through the window. He cups a hand over his eyes to block glare.

He knocks on the door a third time. Then he reaches and tries the knob. The door opens onto a deep space before him, cool, scented. He stands looking and listening.

He turns and gestures to Agata. She steps up beside him. "Hurry," he says indicating inside.

The front room is very dark for eyes just in from the blinding sunshine. A thick knotted rug covers a flagstone floor. They become aware of blocky wooden furniture with armrests broad as tables, chartreuse light in corners, the vague smell of meals past. They stand for a moment.

Dan says, "Hello?" There is no sound.

They step forward toward a doorway with an adzed beam lintel. Ahead, a tiled kitchen angles away. A window opens onto a small leafy space beyond, where mint and oregano grow in pots along the sill.

Agata is ahead of Dan. She enters the kitchen and then stops suddenly. He bumps into her.

Around the corner, leaning against the counter, stands a man. His arms are folded. His hair is black, as is his mustache.

Dan and Agata stand very still. All eye each other.

At this moment another man emerges quietly from a dark hallway to the left. He is dressed in a grey suit. He has a hand inside his unbuttoned jacket.

But the man with the mustache turns to the man in the suit and slowly shakes his head, raising a palm to signify calm. Then he turns back to Dan and Agata and straightens from the counter. He is not as tall as Dan. He steps forward watching them. His eyes are dark, crystalline.

He slowly lifts a hand to Dan to shake. "I'm Nikolai Obli. With Interpol."

Dan reaches also slowly and takes his hand and they shake once.

"I thought so," Dan says.

Agata swivels very gradually and looks at Dan.

"I'm with a branch of the agency that specializes in art theft. You must be Daniel Durand. And you must be Agata Svendson," Nikolai says, turning to her and extending his hand again.

Just then a third man emerges from the hallway behind the man in the grey suit who has re-straightened his jacket. He is slight and elegant, with silver hair and similarly gray eyes, wearing a soft nailhead jacket and pink silk tie.

"Henri," Agata says.

"Agata," Henri says. His voice pings.

"I always did enjoy a party," Dan says.

Nikolai says, "Your email to Interpol didn't specify that you were coming to the place you advised us about. But we surmised. A lookout on the street below relayed to us that you had arrived." He speaks English in an accent from the Caucasus wrung through Paris.

Dan nods. "Did you find the paintings?"

Nikolai tilts his head slightly. He stands before Dan and Agata for a few moments, seemingly considering, evaluating. Agata looks from Dan to Henri and back. Then Nikolai gestures to the group to move into the front room. As the three of them do, he steps into an adjoining pantry.

Dan and Agata stand before a sofa. The man in the grey suit waits nearby. His glances are careful. An awkward moment drags by.

Agata starts to say something to Henri but stops as Nikolai steps back through the doorway with a round bundle retrieved from the pantry. The bundle is wrapped in a sheet. He lays the bundle baby-like on the sofa. Slowly, he unswaddles it. One by one, he spreads three paintings on the sofa and a longer one on an empty table before the sofa.

"This is the Léger," Nikolai says, gesturing to the painting on the table. He moves a hand over it as if revealing. The painting's colors are muted by the dimness of the room. He pauses, turns to a wall switch for more light.

"This is the Braque. It was one of his later pieces. The Picasso," he says, "is not hugely significant in his *oeuvre*, but it is a fine example of his post-synthetic work. The Modigliani," Nikolai continues, pointing to the last on the sofa, the largest one. "Well, a beautiful example of a Modigliani woman. They're all still in good condition, as far as I can tell, despite their adventures. No holes or scrapes."

Four people stand staring at the four paintings in the shining silence for several minutes, eyes moving between shapes and colors, amplitudes and postures, touches.

"Very different styles, but you can really see the shift from 1906 to about 1922," Nikolai says like a teacher. Dan nods.

From another room in the house, a clock dings. Birds land on roof tiles and their faint scratching filters through. Somewhere, a dog barks.

Dan looks up. "What if someone comes in?" he says.

Nikolai shakes his head. "Interpol obtained a warrant around midnight. It took several hours with the judge, but our Greek office had already been working on it. We arrived in Athens around five this morning. Greek police," he gestures toward the man in the grey suit, "had already secured the building. The lady of the house has been detained."

"I was thinking more of Alvaro Rodriguez."

Nikolai says, "French police arrested Mr. Franco breaking into your daughter's apartment. Your email arrived in time. You were right. He found her address in your notebook. Your wife and daughter left for Switzerland. We then simply waited for Franco to arrive. Danish police arrested Tranchard. We were not sure where he would go, but we had a hunch, so we staked out Agata's aunt's house in Copenhagen."

Henri says, "Agata, I remembered what you had told me, how he would wait for you to go to the café each day. I was worried for her."

"Voilà," Nikolai says. "Tranchard was found sitting outside, just as Henri had described, on the same bench in the same park from which he watched you, Agata. He apparently has not said anything to the police yet. But we suspect his plan was to apply pressure to the two of you. Threats. They wanted to freeze you in place long enough for Alvaro to reclaim his property.

"Do not be concerned that they will be released," he continues. "We have witnesses in Bratislava who can positively connect both men to a body found there, the body of a banker who was reputed to be a collector of stolen artworks. They will turn on Alvaro and he will turn on them."

223

Nikolai places his hands palms together, prayer-like. He says, "And finally, the Italian state police intercepted the man who calls himself Alvaro Rodriguez driving east not long after he crossed the border past Monaco, just above La Mortola. He was speeding through the tunnels and over the bridges. As I understand it, at more than 220 kph in his Maserati with the top down, reckless even for the Grande Corniche. He was apparently planning to drive all the way to Greece. He had lost the Matisse. It was already in the hands of the government in Paris. He didn't intend to lose the others, too."

A long silence ensues, and then Agata slowly swings the little knapsack around, unknots its ties and draws out the black plastic tube missing its end caps. She holds it out toward them.

"Then what's this?" she says in a small voice.

Dan guesses. "That would be the forgery. I was pretty sure they wouldn't hand off the real thing like that. Priceless piece of heritage."

"Of course not," says Nikolai.

"But what I struggled with," Dan says. "is why they would give Agata a forged painting, tell her it's the real thing, and then track it." He turns toward Henri as he states this.

Henri speaks in his quietly-tinseled, cinematic French accent. "Only Agata had seen the Matisse, although we knew where Alvaro was keeping it. We suspected you knew where the rest of the paintings were, Agata. When I let you know that I planned to take the Matisse, you suggested that I bring it to you, that you would hold it for us. This was a flag for us."

She gazes at Henri as he talks. His voice is small and soft, but the room is silent again, void even of bird sounds. The others do not strain to hear him. Dan slowly glances to Agata. Her jaw muscles move as if she is about to speak, but she does not.

"We knew you had been with Alvaro a lot, and had traveled with him. We knew he had taken you to several of his homes. Over the past few months, when you spoke to me of him, you always spoke of the potential for a big story."

Agata's eyes are on Henri's. His eyes sparkle slightly in the meager lamplight. He smiles gently, encouragingly, as he continues.

"Alvaro told me he had instructed you to investigate Mr. Durand, but I gathered that you were spending more time researching Alvaro. You saw something in him, perhaps. You came to know something more than you were telling me. We had gone to the trouble of having the fake created. When we came to believe that Alvaro already had the real Matisse, we saw a second opportunity to use the copy." He gestures to the tube still in Agata's hand. She looks down to it, as do the others.

"Since you were in play, we took a calculated risk. We set up a little sting operation. Rather than just arresting him outright, I removed the real Matisse from Alvaro's apartment. This was intended to make him panic and flee to the other paintings. Simultaneously, I handed the forgery off to you. We followed to see where you would lead. We sought to draw both of you out at the same time." He sweeps a hand in a small motion toward Dan and Agata. He pauses. "I'm sorry," he says, directed to her personally.

Dan says, "When Tranchard's emails became frantic I knew something had changed drastically. When we received messages that seemed deliberately obscured I knew shackles had been slipped. I just didn't know why yet."

Henri nods. "That was why I allowed you to see Agata and me meeting and eventually me handing off the decoy painting. We knew you'd report it to Alvaro. We knew it would trigger him to go after the rest of the paintings. One way or the other, we were going to track someone to the cache."

Nikolai says, "We lost your signal in Macedonia. But then we received Dan's email last night, with the photos, names, addresses, explanations and so forth. The two of you have brought all the pieces together for us. Dan, you solved the puzzle."

"I didn't solve anything," Dan says. "I'm no detective. I'm just a translator."

During this, Agata's face has drifted through a series of expressions, settling finally into a low rose glow. She shakes her head, eyes turning downward to the paintings on the sofa.

"Glad to have been of assistance," she says.

Dan reaches to her. The group in the room watches this tiny gesture of agony.

"In this matter, you haven't done that much illegal," Henri says to Agata. "You were associated with our targets, but mostly you failed to report what you knew. You withheld information. A misdeed, perhaps. They will detain you briefly for entering this house, which is trespassing. That will provide opportunity for our various agencies to complete our debriefs and for you to fill in the rest of the details for us. Everything you have learned over the past year about their organization and activities."

Her eyes have drifted downward but they come up to his again as he speaks. He smiles at her again, once more as if lifting her, steadying her.

"It may be," he says, "that the background of why you were living in Europe to begin with will come to light in the investigations of Alvaro. At one point he told me what he knew about your – how to put it delicately? – indiscretions regarding your past reporting endeavors. This can be navigated," he says. "I will help you."

She shakes her head and slowly raises her hands helplessly as Dan saw her do when he first exposed his dismay to her in the bar in Dubrovnik.

"Also," Henri clears his throat, and she looks at him, "it would be nice to spend just a little more time chatting with you. With the strain of all this behind us."

"However, Mr. Durand," Nikolai says, turning to Dan, "I regret to remind you that you have a different circumstance. We understand there is a matter of an extradition warrant still on the books for a felony in Canada. Our colleagues there have asked us to direct you their way."

He counts on fingers as he continues.

"Then, there is a problem with your immigration status, plus the Macedonian border police are annoyed because someone matching your description tried to enter their country with a stolen passport, but fled before they could detain you, and a few other smaller offenses have surfaced. For instance, it seems you have little regard for motor vehicle regulations. I think we can straighten out the trivial issues on your behalf, as a token of our goodwill for your assistance. But I see no way around your appointment in Canada."

"That's okay," Dan says. "I was headed there anyway."

Paintings secured, the group descends the radiant pathways and steps. Dan and Agata now wear glittery handcuffs, fastened in front. People in the cafés turn to look.

Dan walks beside Nikolai, who carries the wrapped bundle of paintings crosswise. "Why did you toss our room in Ohrid?" Dan asks him.

"Just to scare you a little. We were concerned that you would dawdle with her. She's worth dawdling over. We needed you to move along. Reports from Madrid were that Alvaro was preparing to run."

"Your accent. Sevastopol?"

"Not far from there. Yevpatoria. You have been to Crimea?" Dan shakes his head. "But I hope to visit one day."

Behind them, Agata walks beside Henri. "If you suspected me, why didn't you say so? I would have broken down," she says to him.

"My friend, you're not the only one with ambitions." Henri says this gently. He has taken the sunglasses from her knapsack and he gently places them on her face since she is squinting in the brilliance. He takes her arm as they navigate crumbling steps.

Back on the side street, the mix of police discuss transportation, talk on phones. Hands still cuffed, Dan digs awkwardly in a jacket pocket. He hands the motorcycle key to a uniformed man who starts the Ducati and adjusts the mirrors, revs the engine just a little. The bike is dirt-crusted from its travels. Dan smiles at the sound, shakes his head.

He and Agata wait in the shade of a high wall a few steps from the group of police. They face each other. They reach and touch each other encouragingly. She takes his hands and holds them, both pairs of wrists jingling together in cuffs.

"There's still a book in it for you," Dan says. "Though maybe not with the conclusion you were hoping for. But when does the conclusion ever match the dream?"

"I'm no *femme fatale*," Agata says, "I hope you don't think that." Her face is square, resolute, as he first saw it.

"Not sure about that. You are technically a *femme*, after all. And you must admit quite *fatale*. But *fatale* in the positive sense."

She grins at him. "Luckily, we're small fish," she says.

"Small fish with dignity," he says.

"What about Angelique? Is she going to be okay?"

"I think she's fine. At the moment, she's sitting in her boyfriend's castle up in Gstaad surrounded by Lalique crystal and security guards. She'll be great so long as there's a gym. For her, the world's problems burn away with each flex of her muscles. She's wired that way. People like her are self-repairing, which is nice because we worry about them less. When I can, I'll help her with the divorce so she can move along. I wish her the best."

Agata asks, "What are you going to do?"

"You mean after they deal with me in Canada? When the balance sheet is cleared, I think I'll come back to Europe. I cannot seem to separate myself from the beauty and tragedy. Once an expatriate, always an expatriate."

He pauses. He muses.

"Then I think possibly I'll situate somewhere to the east. Maybe Bulgaria. Find a job teaching in a little college with old stone towers and 18th-century trees and odd fountains and cobblestone pathways trod by people who spoke dead languages. Long summer evenings and good coffee shops where I can settle in a corner and read. A crossroads of ancient tongues. Someplace from which it's not too arduous to visit my daughter occasionally, or she can visit me, if she wants. I think she will."

"I was thinking – you've lived up to your personal code," she says.

Dan searches Agata's face. "What are you going to do now?"

"I'm going home," she says. "I can start over. Like you." They watch the police crowding and discussing. "What they need," Agata suggests, "is a few more cars cramming into this street. I don't think they've completely blocked it off yet."

"Are you afraid of the people you sent to prison? You now have enemies in Europe and in America. You're broadening your scope."

"Not so much anymore," she says. "Something has changed over the past year, capped off by this run with you. Something has opened up, grown stronger than I ever thought it could. I can take it. I can resist. I've learned something from you. First, I'm going back to New York and own up to what I did. Set the record straight. Then, assuming I survive all of that, maybe I'll move out to Seattle or Portland for a while. Perhaps get a sailboat and anchor in some back bay in the San Juans. Shelter from the rain and write my book."

"A sailboat. I know how to work those," Dan says.

"That's the idea." She reaches up with handcuffed hands and removes her sunglasses and angles a glance up at him, squinting because the sun arcs over the wall behind him, backlighting.

"Solitude and resistance. The modern condition," he says.

"Truth and trust. The condition I'm aiming for."

"You know, those two words are etymologically related and symbiotic. Ironic, in our current political world."

"Of course you would know that," Agata says.

"Are you making fun of me?"

"I'm admiring you. What will happen to you in Canada?"

He shrugs. "Perjury is potentially fourteen years. I don't know what they will do with me. Hopefully less. Hopefully a lot less. I was trying to jail a killer, after all. I'm not dangerous. I meant well, in a clumsy sort of way. On the other hand, I was a sworn officer of the law. And I've been evading fate, if there is such a thing, for a long time. We'll just have to wait and watch how the ball clatters down through the pegs. With a good lawyer, I'll be out in a year. Possibly just probation."

Agata asks, "If you have a felony on your record, can you get a passport? Travel is so important to you."

"It's up to the judge. I think they would generally deny a passport only if someone was a travel risk. There, too, a good

230

lawyer will be crucial. Good lawyers cost money, though. Angelique may help me there. She's always offered."

"I think my father left me a small fortune. Not sure where it is. When I ran from the *Times*, my family's lawyers and the lawyers for my father's foundation were still sorting things out. But if there's any money lying around for me, I will pay for your lawyer. I'll buy you a lawyer. A squad of them. You can dress them in little grey suits and set them up in cute courtroom poses." She grins up at him.

"I am going to miss you," he says.

Her grin cants. V-shaped lines form in her forehead. "It's so hard to say goodbye like this. Like this," she repeats, glancing down at their wrists in shining cuffs. When she looks back up, she emits a small, abrupt sound somewhere between a squeak and a cry, an intake of breath.

"Come and find me," Dan says. "I'd like that."

"How will I know where?"

"You're a researcher. You'll manage," he says, and smiles.

Discussion has concluded among the group of police and agents. A television crew has arrived, presumably tipped by someone on the Athens force. A man pushes a microphone toward police. The camera turns toward Dan and Agata.

"You're right," Dan says, "the sensation begins. Better get on with that book."

An Athens officer in blue and white steps up and takes Agata by an elbow and turns her and leads her gently toward a car that has maneuvered into the narrow lane. She looks back once at Dan.

He stands still in the sun, tall against the wall. He smiles at her.

With the sun at this morning angle, there are no shadows in his face. Agata sees this, and smiles back happily.

CHAPTER 38

ATHENS
1 December, Friday

Daniel David Durand stands at the boarding gate for Air Canada flight 1716 from Athens to Montreal. He leans against a broad stainless pillar. He's wearing jeans, his best remaining t-shirt and the black jacket he bought in Kotor. He wears the shoes he bought in Madrid, now rain-stained and road-scuffed from their travels. He also wears orange plastic handcuffs, fastened in front and affixed to a plastic waist belt, but not uncomfortably.

Near him, three people converse: a member of the Greek Immigration Department, a French Interpol agent in a suit and open collar, and a young Canadian flight attendant, the purser on this flight. They are speaking among themselves in English, but with some difficulty.

The Greek has such a profound accent that no one, possibly even the speaker himself, can understand. The Interpol agent speaks better English, except for an ample salting of incorrect words that throw his listeners. For instance, he substitutes settee for seat, and pronounces it *satay*. The flight attendant keeps asking questions in her very quick youthful English which bursts in staccato phrases. She grows confused. She seems agitated.

Dan leans forward and says, "Excuse me. May I be of assistance?"

He speaks to the Greek for a minute, asks several questions in Greek. Then he turns to the Frenchman and asks more questions in French. He talks to the flight attendant next, clarifies a couple of points about the row assignment and the placement of the prisoner and the route to the bathrooms, mealtimes.

There is more conversation, a few more points to be ironed out. The three of them stand around him a little closer, smiling now, touched suddenly with a hint of gratitude.

Boarding begins. After the first-class customers have passed through, Dan is requested to take his seat in the last row of the far cabin. He walks to the gate before the queued mass of quiet passengers watching him. The security agent checking passports waves him by without eye contact. He walks through the doorway under a lighted sign stating Montreal with his escort, the Interpol agent, following.

Down the tube of the jetway he strides slowly, thoughtfully, though not discontentedly. His face illuminates from below. His features are modern now, no longer medieval.

The jetway operator has parked the mouth of the ramp a few centimeters from the fuselage of the plane. A gap encircles the exit of the tube at the step into the dark core of the vehicle.

Mediterranean sun blazes outside. It heats the downward-sloping jetway, redolent of travelers, of laundry washed and unwashed, places visited, deodorant. The Air Canada plane's fuselage is painted glossy. The morning sun slopes at such an angle that it deflects off the plane, creating a corona around the end of the long dim tunnel ahead: blinding white.

Dan strides slowly downhill, toward the brilliant portal.

Inveterate wanderer PETER ANDERSON has visited more than 60 countries, including extensive travels in all corners of Europe. His sharp observational skills bring depth to his writing about distant lands and keen insight about the people encountered along the way. A lifelong learner and reader, Anderson lives in eastern Idaho at the foot of the Grand Teton range amid a personal library of more than 7,500 volumes. His essays and non-fiction work have appeared in regional and national publications over the previous 30 years. *Follower* is the first installment of the *Expatriate Trio*.

———————————— ACKNOWLEDGMENTS ————————————

I am truly grateful for the assistance received from several readers and friends, but especially Blaire Kribs and Muffy Mead-Ferro. Of course, the editorial assistance of Jeanne Anderson and Rick and Rosemary Ardinger has been invaluable. I'm also indebted to my first true writing teacher, John Edgar Wideman, whose comments still guide me after four decades.

———————————— A BIT OF ART HISTORY ————————————

In the wee hours of May 20, 2010, a French art thief named Vjeran Tomic, known to media and police as "Spider Man" for his building-scaling skills, slipped through a glassed and iron-grated bay window and entered the gloomy galleries of the Musée d'Art Moderne, across the river from la Tour Eiffel. He took advantage of apparently lackadaisical guard routines and an alarm system that was known to be defective. He had been hired by a cohort to steal a single painting, *Still Life with Candlestick* by Fernand Léger. The Léger quickly bagged, Tomic could not resist opportunity. He also took *Dove with Green Peas* by Pablo Picasso, *Woman with Fan* by Amedeo Modigliani, *Olive Tree near l'Estaque* by Georges Braque and *Pastoral* by Henri Matisse. He then slipped back through the window he had entered and carried the paintings in a canvas bag to an art dealer, who, expecting only the Léger, expressed shock and perhaps delight at seeing the rest.

At their trial in early 2017, one of Tomic's co-defendants – art traffickers who had participated in the plot — claimed that he panicked as police closed in and threw the paintings away. However, neither the court, nor art-theft experts, nor, for that matter, any of the other four defendants in the affair, believe this happened. Many suspect the paintings have been transported out of France and remain in private collections to this day, perhaps scattered, perhaps together.

FROM
LIMBERLOST PRESS

Waltzing with the Captain: Remembering Richard Brautigan

Memoir by Greg Keeler

Teaching English at Montana State University, poet Greg Keeler met *Trout Fishing in America* author Richard Brautigan in 1978 and opened a wildly memorable chapter in his own life. Having secluded himself on a 40-acre ranch in Paradise Valley, Montana, in the mid-1970s, Brautigan needed a friend with whom to talk and carouse. Attracted like a moth to the flame, Keeler became that friend and confidant, driver and clumsy co-conspirator in a number of escapades on the trout streams and rivers, bars and cafes, and along the back roads of Montana. Together they waltzed through many late nights, until Brautigan took his own life in Bolinas, California, in 1984.

Decades after Brautigan's death, Greg Keeler recalls those times with haunting clarity. Illustrated with photographs and the author's cartoon-like drawings at the head of every chapter, *Waltzing with the Captain* is darkly funny and poignant in its revealing portrait of an important contemporary American writer, and in its candid story of an often-tested and bumbling friendship between two poets.

Quality 170-page paperback original, $15 (plus $3 S & H)

Of Your Passage, O Summer

Poems by John Haines

Of Your Passage, O Summer is a collection of poems from the late-1950s and early-1960s thought lost long ago, then found decades later and published in honor of the poet's 80th year. Haines, the poet laureate of Alaska, homesteaded in the wilderness 68 miles south of Fairbanks, working and living off the land. Written in relative isolation, the poems reflect news of the time—the Cuban missile crisis, the fear of confrontation with the Soviet Union, the threat of nuclear annihilation, the early stages of the Vietnam War.

Influenced by his readings of classical Chinese poets, Haines' poems quietly confront great questions about the very nature of existence, a plea for survival from a solitary survivor on a vast, beautiful, lonely and formidable landscape. Haines dedicates the book "to the time, the place, and the life lived — that which gave me the poems — and now to the reader of them."

Of Your Passage, O Summer is letterpress printed on Mohawk Supertine paper, each copy sewn by hand into Rising Stonehenge wrappers in an edition of 500 copies.

Limited Edition: $15 (plus $3 S & H)

ALSO FROM
LIMBERLOST PRESS

Margaret Aho: *The Only Light We Read By*
Sherman Alexie: *Dangerous Astronomy*
Sandy Anderson: *Jeanne Was Once a Player of Pianos*
Glenn Balch: *The Christmas Horse*
David Beisly-Giuotto: *Sawtooth Country*
Kenneth W. Brewer: *Small Scenes*
B. J. Buckley: *Spaces Both Infinite and Eternal*
Hayden Carruth: *Faxes to William*
Chris Dempsey: *Winter Horses*
Edward Dorn: *Chemo Sábe*
Jennifer Dunbar Dorn: *Galactic Runaway*
Bruce Embree: *Beneath the Chickenshit Mormon Sun*
Lawrence Ferlinghetti: *The Street's Kiss*
Gary Gildner: *The Birthday Party*
Gary Gildner: *The Swing*
Allen Ginsberg: *Mind Writing Slogans*
Shaun T. Griffin: *Driving the Tender Desert Home*
Gerald Grimmett: *The Ferry Woman*
Chuck Guilford: *What Counts*
John Haines: *Of Your Passage, O Summer*
Gary Holthaus: *An Archaeology of Home*
Byron Johnson: *Poetic Justice*
Greg Keeler: *Almost Happy*
Greg Keeler: *A Mirror to the Safe*
Greg Keeler: *Waltzing With the Captain*
Alex Kuo: *This Fierce Geography*
Alan Minskoff: *Blue Ink Runs Out on a Partly Cloudy Day*
Alan Minskoff: *Point Blank: The DJ Poems*
Ray Obermayr: *Time's Up?*

THE **LIMBERLOST**
REVIEW
A LITERARY JOURNAL OF THE MOUNTAIN WEST

An anthology that features some of the best writing from the Mountain West and beyond, including poetry, fiction, memoir, essay, translation, commentary about books we come back to again, interviews, artwork, and more.

For books or copies of THE LIMBERLOST REVIEW, email editors@limberlostpress.com or visit www.limberlostpress.com
17 Canyon Trail, Boise, Idaho 83716

Follower is set in a classic serif typeface, *Goudy Old Style*. It was designed by Frederic W. Goudy for American Type Founders (ATF) in 1915. Goudy was a master of type design in the first half of the twentieth century in America. *Goudy Old Style* was inspired by sixteenth-century Italian printing. Goudy added distinctive calligraphic elements to his typeface, including diamond-shaped dots, beautiful ligatures, and graceful italic letters.

Book design by Meggan Laxalt Mackey, Studio M Publications & Design, Boise, Idaho. Cover, chapter head, and endsheet illustrations by Meghan Hanson and Kathleen Hanson, Stevensville, Montana. Map illustration by Erin Ann Jensen, Vancouver, Washington. Printed and bound by Sheridan Books, Chelsea, Michigan. Published in 2020 by Rick and Rosemary Ardinger, Limberlost Press, Boise, Idaho.